"Social life is essentially practical. All mysteries which lead theory astray into mysticism find their rational solution in human practice and in the comprehension of this practice."

KARL MARX, EIGHTH THESIS ON FEUERBACH

"[Marx] discovered the special law of motion governing the present-day capitalist mode of production, and the bourgeois society that this mode of production has created. The discovery of surplus value suddenly threw light on the problem, in trying to solve which all previous investigations, of both bourgeois economists and socialist critics, had been groping in the dark. . . .

Marx was before all else a revolutionist. . . . Fighting was his element. And he fought with a passion, a tenacity and a success such as few could rival. . . .

And, consequently, Marx was the best hated and most calumniated man of his time. Governments, both absolutist and republican, deported him from their territories. Bourgeois, whether conservative or ultra-democratic, vied with one another in heaping slanders upon him. . . .

His name will endure through the ages, and so also will his work."

FREDERICK ENGELS' SPEECH AT THE GRAVE OF KARL MARX HIGHGATE CEMETERY, LONDON, MARCH 17, 1883

Marx's *Capital*

Marx's *Capital*

An Introductory Reader

VENKATESH ATHREYA

VIJAY PRASHAD

JAYATI GHOSH

R. RAMAKUMAR

PRASENJIT BOSE

T. JAYARAMAN

PRABHAT PATNAIK

Offset edition first published in January 2011.
Digital print edition, January 2020.

LeftWord Books
2254/2A Shadi Khampur
New Ranjit Nagar
New Delhi 110008
INDIA

www.leftword.com

LeftWord Books is a division of
Naya Rasta Publishers Pvt. Ltd.

ISBN 978-93-80118-00-0

Contents

Publisher's Note

Each of the essays in this volume is a commissioned piece, written especially for new readers of *Capital*. In a volume of this kind, it is inevitable — indeed, it is desirable — that some basic formulations be stated explicitly, which readers with some background of the subject may find preliminary. However, each of the authors has taken care to not limit him/herself to only preliminary explication of concepts, and has endeavoured to go into matters of advanced theory. The volume as a whole also has a broadly similar trajectory — the first couple of essays set the foundation, the middle four essays graduate from basic concepts to theoretical discussion and debates, and the last essay does not go into basic concepts at all, but applies the method of *Capital* to theorise about contemporary capitalism.

No single volume can do complete justice to the entire range of subjects covered by Marx in *Capital*, and this volume is no exception. However, as stated above, the volume is an introductory reader, meant to only equip new readers with the basic conceptual keys that could unlock the vast treasure trove of Marx's analysis and insights.

Reading *Capital*

Venkatesh Athreya

Reading *Capital* changed my life.

It happened almost, but not quite, by accident. I had completed my bachelor's degree in Chemical Engineering from a 'prestigious' Indian institute in 1969 and had, to every one's surprise, chosen to pursue doctoral studies in economics at a US university. The student movement against the US aggression in Viet Nam was developing powerfully at the university where I had enrolled for my Ph.D. But the courses I had to study as part of my doctoral programme in economics did not provide any explanation for such important questions as to why the world's most powerful nation was engaged in a war of aggression against a tiny third world country. It was then that I stumbled upon a study group negotiating Karl Marx's *Das Kapital*. You may wonder why this is even worth a mention when the book under reference is a very difficult book on economics written in the 1850s and 1860s, which many think is obsolete and irrelevant. But I had by this time realized that mainstream economics offered no credible explanation of the unjust world we lived in, and I was willing to join the study circle. The next six months changed my life entirely.

I read *Das Kapital* in English, and the first time as part of a study circle of ten persons, most of whom were doctoral students at the university from various social science disciplines. At first, I found I had to read the text very carefully, as each sentence was significant in a different way each time I read it. Slowly, I realized that the manner of Marx's argument was relentlessly logical, and I began to enjoy the book a great deal, as an engineer with an inclination to analytical argumentation. As I read the book over and over again over the next several semesters of my stay in the university, I began to see something else in *Capital*. Even in translation, *Capital* read like poetry! So immense was Marx's scholarship, apart from his acute grasp of political economy arising from his basic theoretical framework of dialectical and historical materialism, that the pages of *Capital*, in the middle of abstract argument, would be enlivened by an apt quotation from Shakespeare or Goethe! The other striking aspect of Marx's style of writing was the sharp sense of humour, with devastating sarcasm marking his references to some bourgeois economists like Nassau Senior and Jeremy Bentham who were apologists for the capitalist system.

What did I, an engineering graduate trained in mathematical economics, learn from *Capital*? First, I learnt that to understand a society and its dynamics, one needed to look at it in historical perspective. Second, the basic determinants of the dynamics of a society lay in the manner in which the means of production were owned and the relationship between the direct producers and the means of production. Third, the capitalist mode of production in essence is based upon (*i*) a separation of the direct producers (working people) from the means of production and their transformation into free wage labourers at one pole, (*ii*) the transformation of the means of production into the private monopoly/property of a class of capitalists at the other pole, and (*iii*) the logic of relentless pursuit of profit on private account, with all production taking place on private account for sale in markets with a view to profit. Marx demonstrates that this profit-driven system is necessarily expansionist, both in terms of geography and in terms of the range of activities that can be brought under the drive of profit. To read the discussion on the circuit of capital as well as the last part entitled 'the modern theory of colonization' in the first volume of *Capital* is to understand the inherently globalizing nature of capitalism. After all, if the sole goal is profit, why should the pursuit of it be confined to one part of the world or only one set of activities? If making money is the name of the game, why not make it in any manner possible, be it running a factory or a self financing college or worse! Surely, business ethics is an oxymoron, a contradiction in terms! Marx's analysis of the capitalist mode of production and its inherent logic enables one to understand colonial expansion and what Lenin later called the system of imperialism with its global expansion and colonization and enslavement of people all over the world.

Marx's analysis in *Capital* brings out the contradictory nature of capitalism as an economic system. On the one hand, both the competition among capitalists and the struggle between the class of capitalists and the class of workers leads to constant mechanization and automation of production, leading to the rapid development of society's productive forces. On the other hand, these very processes, which are part of the pursuit of profit, limit the growth of consuming power in society by creating increasing unemployment and limiting wage increases over time, and by dispossessing producers in pre-capitalist sectors/economies. Periodically, this contradiction between the rapidly growing producing power of capitalist society and the much slower growth of consuming power, results in a demand crisis, with massive amounts of goods and services remaining unsold and large numbers of people thrown into the ranks of the unemployed. Capitalism being an unplanned and anarchic system, sectoral imbalances can also lead to overall economic crisis. Thirdly, in so far as technological progress is also unplanned at the systemic level, the rise in productivity does not always keep pace with the increase in the underlying investments that make the technological progress possible, leading to a tendency for the rate of profit to fall now and then. All these and other factors historically have made the capitalist system prone to large fluctuations in output and employment, causing immense misery to working people. Besides, the competition among capitalists and rivalry among capitalist nation states on a global scale led, in the twentieth century, to two global wars resulting in misery for millions of people and massive profits for a handful of large corporations. Currently, the world is in the midst of a global recession, whose predicted recovery is unlikely to make any dent on unemployment until 2011.

The current global crisis of climate change has brought into sharp focus the wasteful ways of the global capitalist system driven by relentless pursuit of profit and the accompanying disregard for the environment and the fate of future generations. It was Marx's *Capital* that boldly proclaimed the historically inevitable demise of the capitalist mode of production in the face of the apparently triumphant march of capitalism across the globe that seemed self-evident to defenders of the capitalist system in the nineteenth century. The twentieth century experience showed that vast numbers of people across the world, both in the industrially advanced countries and in the colonized countries, were ready to revolt against the inequities of the capitalist system. The first decade of the present century has once again highlighted the inability of the capitalist system, despite enormous advances in science and technology, to solve the basic problems facing humanity, including the rather modest goals of food, shelter, clothing, education and health for all. Marx's analysis in *Capital*, and his prognosis of the system of capitalism promoting the accumulation of wealth at one pole and misery at the other, remains relevant and inspiring.

IS *CAPITAL* TOO DAUNTING TO READ?

There is a perception, even among activists on the political Left including those in academia, that *Capital* is a very difficult, if not impossible, book to read. I disagree. It is of course true that *Capital* demands of its readers a certain level of commitment in the sense that the reader must work his or her way through the often complicated logic of its arguments. But one would expect this of any serious analytical work. The difference, in the case of *Capital* is, if anything, to its advantage, since reading *Capital* can be immensely, immeasurably, rewarding.

    Capital presupposes a strong degree of engagement of the reader with its primary concern: analysis of the capitalist mode of production with a view to laying bare its inner dynamic and contradictions, summarized in the term 'laws of motion of capitalism'. Any such analysis, as historical materialism teaches us, must necessarily develop historically specific analytical concepts and categories relevant to the mode of production being analysed. In doing so, a certain level of abstraction is inevitable. Marx himself puts the matter in the following words:

> In the analysis of economic forms, moreover, neither microscopes nor chemical reagents are of use. The force of abstraction must replace both. (*Capital*, I, p. 19)[1]

Marx also makes the point that the proposition that every beginning is difficult 'holds in all sciences', while referring to the apparent difficulty in understanding the first three chapters of the first volume of *Capital* dealing with the concepts of 'commodity' and 'value'. The important thing is not to be intimidated by the opening chapters of the first volume of *Capital*. There is no particular order in which the book *has* to be read, and each reader should decide, based on his or her prior preparation and inclination the sequence of reading.

    Readers who enjoy a historical account more readily than abstract analysis may want to begin with the last part of the first volume of *Capital* that deals with the process of 'primary' or 'primitive' accumulation of capital. This part, in eight crisp chapters or around seventy pages of vivid prose, explains how the capitalist mode of production emerged and how the main classes of this mode of production emerged on the historical stage in the country of birth of modern capitalism, namely England of the seventeenth to the nineteenth centuries. Particularly striking is the chapter on the historical tendency of the capitalist mode of production which contains the following brilliant description of the logical end of this mode:

> . . . as soon as the labourers are turned into proletarians, their means of labour into capital, as soon as the capitalist mode of production stands on its own feet, then the further socialization of labour and further transformation of the land and other means of production into socially exploited and, therefore, common means of production, as well as the further expropriation of private proprietors, takes a new form. That which is now to be expropriated is no longer the labourer working for himself, but the capitalist exploiting many labourers. This expropriation is accomplished by the action of the immanent laws of capitalistic production itself, by the centralization of capital. One capitalist always kills many. Hand in hand with this centralization, or this expropriation of many capitalists by few, develop, on an ever-extending scale, the cooperative form of the labour process, the conscious technical application of science, the methodical cultivation of the soil, the transformation of the instruments of labour into instruments of labour only usable in common, the economizing of all means of production by their use as the means of production of combined, socialised labour, the entanglement of all peoples in the net of the world-market, and with this, the international character of the capitalistic regime. Along with the constantly diminishing number of the magnates of capital, who usurp and monopolise all advantages of this process of transformation, grows the mass of misery, oppression, slavery, degradation, exploitation; but with this too grows the revolt of the working-class, a class always increasing in numbers, and disciplined, united, organized by the very mechanism of the process of capitalist production itself. The monopoly of capital becomes a fetter upon the mode of production, which has sprung up and flourished along with, and under it. Centralisation of the means of production and socialization of labour at last reach a point where they become incompatible with their capitalist integument. This integument is burst asunder. The knell of capitalist private property sounds. The expropriators are expropriated. (*Capital*, I, pp. 714–15)[2]

Militants of the working class movement may find Parts III, IV and V of *Capital* (volume I), which deal with the production of absolute and relative surplus value more immediately interesting than the rather abstract opening chapters. The tenth chapter entitled 'The Working Day' will be especially relevant for militants in the third world countries such as India where the length of the working day still varies greatly across industries and sectors, and is generally unconscionably long, including in some very modern, 'high-tech' segments. This chapter is a real *tour de force*, covering a vast ground of concrete history — including legislative history — with a constant focus on the basic class question at hand, namely the struggle between the insatiable appetite of capital for surplus value and the gradually emerging resistance of the working class to gross exploitation. Here is the core idea of this chapter in Marx's own words:

> The establishment of a normal working-day is the result of centuries of struggle between capitalist and labourer. The history of this struggle shows two opposed tendencies . . . Whilst the modern Factory Acts compulsorily shortened the working-day, the earlier statutes tried to lengthen it by compulsion . . . It takes centuries ere the 'free' labourer, thanks to the development of capitalistic production agrees, i.e., is compelled by social conditions, to sell the whole of his active life, his very capacity for work, for the price of the necessaries of life, his birthright for a mess of pottage. (*Capital*, I, pp. 257–58)

As he brings the chapter on the working day to a close, Marx reminds us of the crucial transformation that occurs once the worker has entered into an employment contract with the capitalist and entered the work premises, and its implications for the working class:

> It must be acknowledged that our labourer comes out of the production process other than he entered. In the market, he stood as the owner of the commodity 'labour power' face to face with other owners of commodities, dealer against dealer. The contract by which he sold to the capitalist his labour power proved, so to say, in black and white that he disposed of himself freely. The bargain concluded, it is discovered that he was no 'free agent', that the time for which he is free to sell his labour power is the time for which he is forced to sell it . . . the labourers must put their heads together, and, as a class, compel the passing of a law, an all-powerful social barrier that shall

prevent the workers from selling, by voluntary contract with capital, themselves and their families into slavery and death. In place of the pompous catalogue of the 'inalienable rights of man' comes the modest Magna Charta of a legally limited working-day . . . (*Capital*, I, pp. 285–86)

It is interesting to note that while Marx was writing in the 1860s of the need to limit the working day in the context of Great Britain, our worthy captains of industry in twenty-first century 'globalizing' India, demand freedom from all labour legislation and raise the slogan of the need for 'flexible labour', supported in this demand by our imported and home-grown academic worthies serving their interests in and out of government.[3]

Engineers and technologists will find absolutely fascinating Marx's treatment in Chapters XII, XIII and XIV, respectively, of cooperation, of division of labour and manufacture, and of machinery and modern industry. Marx treats the reader to a detailed discussion of technical matters as they pertain to industrial production in a manner that is readily comprehensible. This will engage the engineer and the technologist. But Marx does something far more remarkable. He never loses sight of the larger context within which the technical discussion has to be placed so that it can be correctly understood. That context is one of social and historical transformation, and of the contradictory effects of scientific and technological advance under the capitalist mode of production, especially the deleterious impact of mechanization on the worker under capitalism. In an overall positive summing up of the historical role of modern industry, Marx makes the following important observations:

Modern industry never looks upon and treats the existing form of a process as final. The technical basis of that industry is therefore revolutionary, while all earlier modes of production were essentially conservative. By means of machinery, chemical processes and other methods, it is continually causing changes not only in the technical basis of production, but also in the functions of the labourer, and in the social combinations of the labour-process. At the same time, it thereby also revolutionises the division of labour within the society, and incessantly launches masses of capital and of workpeople from one branch of production to another. But if modern industry, by its very nature, therefore necessitates variation of labour, fluency of function, universal mobility of the labourer, on the other hand, in its capitalistic form, it reproduces the old division of labour with its ossified particularisations. We have seen how this absolute contradiction between the technical necessities of modern industry, and the social character inherent in its capitalistic form, dispels all fixity and security in the situation of the labourer; how it constantly threatens, by taking away the instruments of labour, to snatch from his hands his means of subsistence, and, by suppressing his detail-function, to make him superfluous. We have seen, too, how this antagonism vents its rage in the creation of that monstrosity, an industrial reserve army, kept in misery in order to be always at the disposal of capital; in the incessant human sacrifices from among the working-class, in the most reckless squandering of labour-power and in the devastation caused by a social anarchy which turns every economic progress into a social calamity. This is the negative side. But if, on the one hand, variation of work at present imposes itself after the manner of an overpowering natural law, and with the blindly destructive action of a natural law that meets with resistance at all points, modern industry, on the other hand, through its catastrophes imposes the necessity of recognising, as a fundamental law of production, variation of work, consequently fitness of the labourer for varied work, consequently the greatest possible development of his varied aptitudes. It becomes a question of life and death for society to adapt the mode of production to the normal functioning of this law. Modern industry, indeed, compels society, under penalty of death, to replace the detail-worker of to-day, grappled by life-long repetition of one and the same trivial operation, and thus reduced to the mere fragment of a man, by the fully developed individual, fit for a variety of labours, ready to face any change of production, and to whom the different social functions he performs, are but so many modes of giving free scope to his own natural and acquired powers. (*Capital*, I, pp. 457–58)

While Marx thus takes a balanced and historically informed view of the role of modern industry, he does not by any means romanticise the actual process of industrial modernization under the aegis of the capitalist mode of production. In an interesting discussion of the relation between modern industry and agriculture, Marx anticipates some of the contemporary ecological concerns. In a typically dialectical assessment of the impact of capitalist industrial modernization on agriculture and the working people in agriculture, here is what Marx has to say:

> Capitalist production completely tears asunder the old bond of union which held together agriculture and manufacture in their infancy. But at the same time it creates the material conditions for a higher synthesis in the future, viz., the union of agriculture and industry on the basis of the more perfected forms they have each acquired during their temporary separation. Capitalist production, by collecting the population in great centres, and causing an ever-increasing preponderance of town population, on the one hand concentrates the historical motive power of society; on the other hand, it disturbs the circulation of matter between man and the soil, i.e., prevents the return to the soil of its elements consumed by man in the form of food and clothing; it therefore violates the conditions necessary to lasting fertility of the soil. By this action it destroys at the same time the health of the town labourer and the intellectual life of the rural labourer. But while upsetting the naturally grown conditions for the maintenance of that circulation of matter, it imperiously calls for its restoration as a system, as a regulating law of social production, and under a form appropriate to the full development of the human race. (*Capital*, I, p. 474)

Marx concludes this discussion thus:

> Moreover, all progress in capitalistic agriculture is a progress in the art, not only of robbing the labourer, but of robbing the soil; all progress in increasing the fertility of the soil for a given time, is a progress towards ruining the lasting sources of that fertility... Capitalist production, therefore, develops technology, and the combining together of various processes into a social whole, only by sapping the original sources of all wealth-the soil and the labourer.[4] (*Capital*, I, pp. 474–75)

CAPITAL AS A DELIGHTFUL READ

Capital is thus not a daunting read. It is, as we can see from the foregoing extracts, a source of valuable knowledge and rich insights that enables us to understand some key aspects of capitalism as a mode of production even today, despite the phenomenal changes that have occurred since the first volume of *Capital* was published, back in 1867. It is perhaps not an exaggeration to say that the ruling classes have also learnt from the superbly incisive analysis of the capitalist mode of production in *Capital.* Bourgeois ideologists, including in academia, have long tried to bury *Capital* by ignoring it. Among mainstream economists, the dominant strategy has been to deny that Marx was a noteworthy economist, but treat him instead as a political propagandist. Forced to reckon with the continuing relevance of Marx in the context of both the real economic crisis of contemporary global capitalism and the crisis of mainstream economic theory in its neoliberal and Keynesian variants, mainstream economists are finding it increasingly difficult to dismiss Marx as either a non-economist or a minor post-Ricardian.[5]

Apart from its importance in providing the reader with valuable insights on the nature and dynamics of the capitalist mode of production, insights which have contemporary relevance, the other important feature of *Capital* that I have been struck by is its method of presentation of arguments. Consider, for instance, what is often seen as a difficult part of *Capital,* namely the first chapter of the first volume which deals with the concept of commodity and develops the category of 'value'. Far from being difficult, the argument in the chapter is systematic and goes through a series of simple logical steps to arrive at a profound understanding of the nature of a commodity. The first section of the chapter develops the point that a commodity — anything produced on private account with a view to sell in a market and not for own use — has two aspects of importance. First, it must be useful to someone in society or else it cannot be exchanged, which means it ceases to be a commodity in effect. This aspect, which Marx terms the use value property of a commodity, is a function of the natural-physical and chemical-properties of the commodity. However, the whole idea of producing something as a commodity is to *sell* it. This implies that a commodity must possess *exchange* value. Marx's central point here is that, while the commodity is thus perceived as having use value and exchange value, the exchange value is only the external appearance, the form of expression as it were, of something deeper. This deeper aspect, that which makes the most different commodities comparable and commensurable, cannot be their *natural* properties since these differ from commodity to commodity, but it is rather a *social* property. The obvious commonness of all commodities is that they are all products of the expenditure of human labour in society. This common property that all commodities have, namely that they are all products of society's labour, is what makes them commensurable, and Marx calls this property 'value'. Now, starting from this carefully built scaffold, he raises a marvellous structure of logical argument in *Capital* that enables him to unravel the inner dynamics of the capitalist mode of production.

A key feature of Marx's method, which *Capital* is suffused with, is that of showing the contradictory character of all the phenomena under investigation. We saw this in the earlier quotation from *Capital* on the historical role of machinery and modern industry. We saw it again in the passage that we quoted on the historical tendency of the capitalist mode of production. The remarkable twenty-fifth chapter in the first volume of *Capital* on 'The General Law of Capitalist Accumulation' is another outstanding example of Marx's method of argument of starting out with simple categories depicting various aspects of the phenomenon under study, and showing the process of their dynamic evolution through the working out of their inherent contradictions. It is of course important to emphasize that the contradictions being discussed by Marx are real ones on the ground and not merely contradictions of the theoretical categories used to represent the real world.

It is, in retrospect, astonishing that Marx managed to make such a deep and profound structure of argument — and several substructures within the overall structure — so eminently readable. One feature of *Capital* that contributes to this readability is that every theoretical argument is immediately illustrated from contemporary history — and in many instances with the events and phenomena of earlier historical epochs as well. Marx makes generous but careful and rigorous use of official records, reports and data sources in illustrating and emphasizing his arguments. But he is careful to keep his structures of argument distinct and analytically valid on their own, even as he uses empirical evidence to illustrate, strengthen and illuminate his arguments. His frequent reference to fine works of literature and appropriate quotes from them relieves the reader struggling with dense arguments from time to time. Consider, for instance, the following passage on the capitalist engaged in the accumulation of capital:

> To accumulate, is to conquer the world of social wealth, to increase the mass of human beings exploited by him, and thus to extend both the direct and the indirect sway of the capitalist.
>
> But original sin is at work everywhere. As capitalist production, accumulation, and wealth, become developed, the capitalist ceases to

be the mere incarnation of capital. He has a fellow-feeling for his own Adam, and his education gradually enables him to smile at the rage for asceticism, as a mere prejudice of the old-fashioned miser. While the capitalist of the classical type brands individual consumption as a sin against his function, and as 'abstinence' from accumulating, the modernised capitalist is capable of looking upon accumulation as 'abstinence' from pleasure. (*Capital*, I, pp. 555–56)

Marx captures this contradiction between wanting to enjoy the good life and the compulsion to accumulate by quoting from Goethe's *Faust*:

Two souls, alas, do dwell with in his breast;
The one is ever parting from the other. (Ibid.)

Marx then elaborates the argument, bringing out the contradictions involved and showing how they change with the dynamics of capitalism in history:

At the historical dawn of capitalist production, — and every capitalist upstart has personally to go through this historical stage — avarice, and desire to get rich, are the ruling passions. But the progress of capitalist production not only creates a world of delights; it lays open, in speculation and the credit system, a thousand sources of sudden enrichment. When a certain stage of development has been reached, a conventional degree of prodigality, which is also an exhibition of wealth, and consequently a source of credit, becomes a business necessity to the 'unfortunate' capitalist. Luxury enters into capital's expenses of representation. Moreover, the capitalist gets rich, not like the miser, in proportion to his personal labour and restricted consumption, but at the same rate as he squeezes out the labour-power of others, and enforces on the labourer abstinence from all life's enjoyments. Although, therefore, the prodigality of the capitalist never possesses the bona fide character of the open-handed feudal lord's prodigality, but, on the contrary, has always lurking behind it the most sordid avarice and the most anxious calculation, yet his expenditure grows with his accumulation, without the one necessarily restricting the other. But along with this growth, there is at the same time developed in his breast, a Faustian conflict between the passion for accumulation, and the desire for enjoyment. (*Capital*, I, pp. 556–57)

The chapters on primitive accumulation, too, contain many such delightful passages, dripping with irony in their relentless expose of capitalist hypocrisy.

A FINAL WORD

So go ahead, have a great read! And, by the way, do not forget to read the prefaces and the after-words to the various editions by Marx and by Engels. Hope you enjoy reading all the three volumes of *Capital* as much as I did — and still do!

NOTES

1 All references to *Capital* are from the LeftWord Books edition, New Delhi, 2010.

2 Brilliant and in some ways evocative of contemporary capitalism as this description is, the actual development of capitalist social formations — as opposed to the immanent tendency of the theoretical construct of the 'capitalist mode of production' — has been very different. An important part of the explanation for this difference rests, of course, with the rise of imperialism as an integral part of the evolution of capitalism. Professor Patnaik's contribution to this volume explores this issue as a whole in depth.

3 See, for instance, successive issues, over the last several years, of the *Economic Survey*, an annual publication of the Ministry of Finance of the Government of India.

4 A good introduction to Marx's perspectives and views on issues of ecology and environment can be found in John Bellamy Foster, *Marx's Ecology* (Monthly Review Press, New York, 2000).

5 The reference here is to David Ricardo, who was regarded, along with Adam Smith, as a classical political economist by Marx. Ricardo's major work is *The Principles of Political Economy and Taxation*. He and Smith, whose classic work *The Wealth of Nations* (1776) is often (and misleadingly) invoked by neoliberals, were the most important economists articulating the views of the emerging class of capitalists during a key phase of Britain's transition to capitalism between the 1770s and the 1830s. Marx regarded both Smith and Ricardo highly, but also provided the most incisive critique of their views. If you courageously manage to read the three volumes of Capital, you can go on to read Marx's magnum opus on the history of economic thought, the three-volume *Theories of Surplus Value*!

Writing *Capital*

Vijay Prashad

> I don't suppose anyone has ever written about 'money' and suffered such a lack of it himself.
>
> — Marx to Engels, January 21, 1859

Karl Marx and his family fled the European continent for London in the autumn of 1849. A decade of mass political unrest fell apart in the face of systematic repression whose crowning moment was the coronation of Prince Louis Napoleon. Marx spent the rest of his life in London working on his magnum opus, the series of books that culminated in his most famous, with the simple title *Capital*. A précis of his argument had already appeared in 1847 in two installments, as *The Poverty of Philosophy* and as lectures to the German Workers' Society (*Wage Labour and Capital*). But these were not sufficiently elaborated as to lay claim to the foundation of a new philosophy of the system. Marx had greater ambitions. He had already figured out the ills of the system (as was clear in the 1848 *Manifesto*), but he had not yet clearly delineated the philosophical underpinnings for his critique. That would take time.

But time was the one thing he could not make. He laboured without pay. That had its costs on him and his family. Jenny von Westphalen, who married Karl in 1843, had influenced Marx's politics in their native Trier. As her biographer put it, Jenny Marx 'shared the misery of his refugee existence, copied his illegible manuscripts, fought off his creditors, prepared his meals and bore him seven children.'[1] Of those seven children, four died before adulthood, and one committed suicide at 43 (that would be Tussy, or Eleanor Marx). The reproduction of the Marx household was always tenuous. It took all the energy of everyone to produce the first volume of *Capital* (1867), which distressed Marx, his family, and his comrade and benefactor Engels. Penury interrupted his work, but this was not the only thing. The other was that Marx had to work out a method to provide his new synthesis. This took him years.

OLD JOB

> I am plagued like Job, though not so God-fearing.
> — Marx, 1858

Karl Marx lived in abject poverty. During his London years, the Marx family went from one slum to another, from Chelsea to Soho, living amidst those whom Marx and his friend Engels characterized as the 'scum, offal, and refuse of all classes'. This *lumpen* or rag proletariat lived around the Marx family, and his household matched, in most particulars, their way of life. The family never had enough money. Starvation was as commonplace as the London rain. Marx's son Edgar kept the creditors away with his cockney outbursts, 'No, Mr. Marx ain't upstairs.' On April 6, 1855, Edgar died in Marx' arms. He was not yet eight. Edgar joined his two siblings in death, Guido (age 1) and Franziska (age 1). After Franziska died in 1852, Marx wrote to Engels on April 14, 'I could not and cannot fetch the doctor because I have no money for the medicine. For the last eight or ten days I have fed my family on bread and potatoes, and today it is still doubtful whether I shall be able to obtain even these.' Death was not inevitable. It came because of the damp, the congestion, the hunger, and the lack of medical care. None of this surprised Engels. In his masterful *Condition of the Working Class in England* (1845), Engels summarized the mortality evidence from England, 'The death-rate is kept so high chiefly by the heavy mortality among young children in the working-class. The tender frame of a child is least able to withstand the unfavorable influences of an inferior lot in life; the neglect to which they are often subjected.' Marx did not simply write from the standpoint of a remote and imaginary working-class. He also wrote from his own experiences.

Money did not come to the Marx household easily. Karl Marx's political work brought in no earnings. He threw himself into the organization of the Communist League and the International Working Men's Association. These flourished as much as possible, but they were not all Marx's political work. He involved himself in the Chartist movement, the Committee of Support for German Political Refugees and the London German Workers' Educational Society. Some money came from Marx's writings for newspapers and journals. His first earnings came in 1842 from *Rheinische Zeitung*, which Marx began to edit not long afterwards. In London, Marx wrote for the Chartist papers (*Notes to the People* and *The People's Paper*), and began a curtailed tenure as the London correspondent for the *New York Daily*

Tribune. Marx wrote on a range of issues, from liberation struggles in Ireland and India to warfare on the continent to the intricacies of English politics. To great effect, Marx employed his formidable grasp of detail and his savage sense of humor. No politician escaped unscathed. When Marx lay ill, Engels helped him with his research, and occasionally, with the writing. Engels also helped with a generous bursary, drawn from his salary at the cotton works of Engels & Ermen. That money went into the trappings of a bourgeois household. Marx could not bear to live without his books, or to have his children bereft of the piano. All his earnings went to build the cultural capital of his family.

Behind the *sturm und drang* of everyday life, Marx contemplated his masterwork. In 1850–51, the Prussian authorities shut down the Communist League. Marx despaired. Not far from his house on Dean Street was the British Museum. It is to this monument of neo-classical construction that Marx repaired daily. Once at the museum, Marx did not stop to examine the Rosetta Stone or the Elgin Marbles. His mission was grander. He requisitioned the Blue Books, the annual volumes that captured the mechanics of the United Kingdom in tables of statistics, as well as the Factory Reports and the Reports on Mines. These gave Marx the massive data-base to fully understand how the economy functioned. Besides these, Marx read and re-read the political economists of the day, most of whose names are long forgotten. On notepaper Marx scribbled his abuses of their errors. One of the most memorable sections is when Marx set Nassau Senior, Professor of Political Economy at Oxford, against Leonard Horner, a factory inspector. Senior had been on the Poor Law Inquiry Commission and the Handloom Weavers Commission. The barons of Manchester commissioned him to do a critique of the government's factory reports. Senior's dispatch irked Horner, who drew upon his experience as the Censor of the Factories to put Senior in his place. '[Horner's] services to the English working-class will never be forgotten', Marx wrote in *Capital* (Chapter 9). Nor should his service to Marx's work be neglected. It was these honest inspectors that provided the raw materials.

It was not easy to get to the library. It had a dress code. In 1852, penury led Marx to the pawnshop. 'A week ago', he wrote to Engels, 'I reached the pleasant point where I was unable to go out for want of the coats I have to pawn' (February 27, 1852). A few months later, the coat returned to the pawnshop because it had to be sold 'in order to buy writing paper'. Marx knew what he was talking about when he wrote the following:

'When the labourer is confronted by the conditions of labour and by the product of labour in the shape of capital, as under the developed capitalist mode of production, he has no occasion to borrow any money as a producer. When he does any money borrowing, he does so, for instance, at the pawnshop to secure personal necessities'(*Capital*, III, Ch. 36, p. 594).[2] No surprise either that the section on fetishism turns to the coat to provide its crowning example (a matter taken up beautifully by Peter Stallybrass in his 1997 essay, 'Marx's Coat').

Without the library, Marx was lost. He turned to the world of fiction. In the evenings, to his children, he read great literary works and recounted the Latin and Greek classics. All these would find their way into *Capital*. For example, in his chapter on 'Machinery and Modern Industry' (Volume I, Chapter 15), Marx turned to the Census of 1861 for his evidence. The Census showed that mechanization in large-scale industry led to mass unemployment. The data did its work. Marx was aware of that. But the political economists who had a soft spot for capitalism had contested that data. Rather than take their shallow arguments seriously, Marx turned to Charles Dickens' *Oliver Twist*, whose lead character Bill Sykes stands in the dock to be tried for stabbing his girlfriend, Nancy. Sykes' absurd defence is the same as that used by the apologists of unemployment. As a riposte it is more effective than anything Marx could have written: 'Gentlemen of the jury, no doubt the throat of this commercial traveler has been cut. But that is not my fault, it is the fault of the knife. Must we, for such a temporary inconvenience, abolish the use of the knife? Only consider! Where would agriculture and trade be without the knife? Is it not as salutary in surgery, as it is knowing in anatomy? And in addition a willing help at the festive board? If you abolish the knife — you hurl us back into the depths of barbarism' (*Capital*, I, p. 416). Deprived of the British Museum, Marx turned to his own collection of popular novels to twist his analytical knife deeper into the logic of capitalist development.

Literature provided Marx with the stinging rebuke. So too did his vast knowledge of the ancient world. He drew upon it not to suggest timelessness, but to play on how old forms make their twisted appearance in bourgeois society. When writing of the capitalist industrial system, Marx let his pen loose,

> Manufacture proper not only subjects the previously independent workman to the discipline and command of capital, but, in addition,

creates a hierarchic gradation of the workmen themselves. While simple co-operation leaves the mode of working by the individual for the most part unchanged, manufacture thoroughly revolutionizes it, and seizes labour-power by its very roots. It converts the labourer into a crippled monstrosity, by forcing his detail dexterity at the expense of a world of productive capabilities and instincts; just as in the States of La Plata they butcher a whole beast for the sake of his hide or his tallow. Not only is the detail work distributed to the different individuals, but the individual himself is made the automatic motor of a fractional operation, and the absurd fable of Menenius Agrippa, which makes man a mere fragment of his own body, becomes realized. (*Capital*, I, p. 340)

This follows an exposition of the division of labour. The detail is important. But so is the style. Agrippa, who died in 493 B.C.E., provided a model of human society that resembles in great part the *varnasharamadharma*. The patricians were the stomach, Agrippa argued, and the plebeians the hands; the latter had to feed the former, and if they failed both would wither. In the preface to *Capital*'s first edition Marx wrote, 'we suffer not only from the living, but from the dead. *Le mort saisit le vij* [The dead clutches onto the living]!' (*Capital*, I, p. 20). So too with the forms of social life. The 'modern evils' of capitalism, he wrote, are molded onto the 'inherited evils'. The point is well made in the text itself by Marx's recourse to historical analogy. This was not to say that nothing had changed between the era of Agrippa and the era of Ancoats, but that the workers who went to work in the cotton mills in the Manchester district of Ancoats suffered a sophisticated system of exploitation intertwined with the degradations of the ancient world. Marx's historical materialism was always aware of the differences of the present alongside the linkages with the past.

The work ate into Marx. It gave him boils. In November 1863, Jenny Marx wrote to Engels of the corporeal costs of the work,

Moor sends you herewith the 'Most Noble Daoud Bey's' *Free Press*. It will amuse you a lot. Karl, alas, cannot write himself. For the past week he has been very unwell and is tied to the sofa. 2 boils appeared on his cheek and back. The one on his cheek responded to the household remedies one normally uses for such things. The other, on his back, has assumed such dimensions and is so inflamed that poor

Moor is enduring the most frightful pain and gets no respite either by day or by night. You can imagine, too, how depressed this business makes him. It seems as though the wretched book will never get finished. It weighs like a nightmare on us all. If only the Leviathan were launched!

Marx is the Moor. The Most Noble Daoud Bey is Marx's peculiar benefactor David Urquhart, whose phlegmatic hatred of Lord Palmerston on Turkish-Russian matters cemented his friendship with Marx (they both took the Turk view). That 'wretched book,' the Leviathan, is *Capital.* In April 1867, as Marx wrote the final pages of *Capital,* he wrote to Engels, keeping him informed about the extreme pain of the work, but not wishing to bore him with reasons for 'the further delay, viz., carbuncles on my posterior and near the **penis**, the final traces of which are now fading but which made it extremely painful for me to adopt a sitting (hence writing) posture. I am *not* taking *arsenic* because it dulls my mind too much and I needed to keep my wits about me at least at those times when writing was possible' (April 2, 1867). A few months later, as the manuscript was on its way, Marx wrote again to his friend, 'I hope the bourgeoisie will remember my carbuncles [boils] until their dying day' (June 22, 1867).

The first volume opened with a preface that began, 'This work, whose first volume I now submit to the public, forms the continuation of my book *Zur Kritik der Politischen Ökonomie,* published in 1859. The long pause between the first part and the continuation is due to an illness of many years' duration, which interrupted my work again and again'(*Capital,* I, p. 18). If Marx had given himself to the side of the bourgeoisie, he would have coats aplenty and his children would have been sent down to the finest preparatory schools and finally, Oxford or Cambridge. He himself would have been a well-paid Don or else a professor at Heidelberg or Munich. The illness that befell Marx and his family was a consequence of his political commitments. It was not Marx's investment to merely interpret the world. He wanted to change it. He paid the price for that choice.

MARX'S CRITIQUE

By the way, I am discovering some nice arguments. For instance, I have overthrown the whole doctrine of profit as it has existed up to now.

— Marx to Engels, January 14, 1858

By the mid-1840s, Marx resolved to write a serious study of political economy. On February 1, 1845, Marx signed a contract with Carl Leske to publish his *Kritik der Politik und National-Ökonomie*. A year later, Leske opted out. Differences arose on political matters, and by 1847, the contract lapsed. Marx had major differences with the principal German socialist thinkers, those whom Engels and he pilloried in *The German Ideology*. That book, written in 1845–46, also failed to find a publisher (it was first published in the Soviet Union in 1932). Ludwig Feuerbach, Bruno Bauer, and Max Stirner were the main intellectuals of the German socialist movement, and neither they, nor their colleagues, liked it when Marx and Engels claimed that *The German Ideology* aimed to uncloak 'these sheep, who take themselves and are taken for wolves; [to show] how their bleating merely imitates in a philosophic form the conceptions of the German middle class.' No wonder that Leske opted out.

Marx had the secret to capitalism figured out by the 1840s and early 1850s. Early evidence that he had uncovered the secret can be glimpsed in Marx's lectures to the German Workers' Society in Brussels from 1847, published in *Neue Rheinishche Zeitung* (1849) and in a pamphlet called *Wage Labour and Capital* (1880). These carry the germ of his interventions. It is here that Marx introduces the idea that under capitalism, workers do not sell their labour, but their labour power. It is as a commodity that this labour power enters the market, and it is as a commodity that it has an impact on wages and prices. The price of things is not determined by the cost of its production, for if that were the case, Marx wrote, it would mean that profit would not exist. Where does profit come from? The answer is not to be found on the surface of economic activity (through the categories of wages and prices). To understand how the economy functions, Marx suggested, one had to delve beneath the surface. Here one would find the mechanism by which the capitalist is able to derive more from the labour power of the worker than the worker would get as wages: it is in the realm of labour power that Marx was able to uncover ideas such as surplus value, a crucial concept for his critique of capitalism. The logic of labour power enabled Marx to predict that society would soon find itself torn into two, between those who have control or own capital and those who are dispossessed from capital. The latter need not only be workers in factories, but they could as well be those who wear white collars and work in office buildings. As he put it, 'the working class gains recruits from the *higher strata of society* also; a mass of petty industrialists and small rentiers are hurled down into its ranks and have nothing better to do than urgently stretch out their arms alongside those of the workers. Thus the forest of uplifted arms demanding work becomes ever thicker, while the arms themselves become ever thinner' (*Wage Labour and Capital*). The secret of the commodity known as labour power would form the basis around the more prosaic sections of the *Manifesto*, written the following year.

The problem for Marx was not what to say. It was how to say it. In other words, the real dilemma was the method, the form. To Ferdinand Lassalle, Marx wrote that 'the material was to hand and all that I was concerned with was the form. But to me, the style of everything I wrote seemed tainted with liver trouble. And I have a two fold motive not for allowing this work to be spoiled on medical grounds.' The first was that he had already given fifteen years to this project, 'the best years of my life'. The second was that Marx felt 'in it an important view of social relations is scientifically expounded for the first time'. It would be a mistake to allow the book to 'be disfigured by the kind of heavy, wooden style proper to a disordered liver' (November 12, 1858). In the 1861–63 *Theories of Surplus Value*, Marx complained about the 'peculiar and necessarily faulty architectonics' of David Ricardo's work. *On the Principles of Political Economy and Taxation* (1817) was not faulty because of a superficial error. Marx saw the fault in 'Ricardo's method of investigation itself and of the definite task which he set himself in his work. It expresses the scientific deficiencies of this method of investigation itself' (Chapter 10). He did not want to replicate such a disaster.

Marx began to write the many versions of this opus from 1857 to 1867. The major unpublished attempt can be read in the massive *Grundrisse*, which Marx told his friend Lassalle is to be called a *Critique of Economic Categories*, 'a critical exposé of the system of the bourgeois economy. It is at once an exposé and, by the same token, a critique of the system. I have very little idea how many sheets the whole thing will amount to' (February 22, 1858). The *Grundrisse* did not see light of day until 1933, when it was published in a limited edition in Moscow (the first mass edition came out in Germany in 1953). In mid-September 1857, Marx drafted his 'Introduction' to the *Grundrisse*, in which he grappled with the complexity of his method (particularly in the section, 'The Method of Political Economy'). It is here that Marx declares that the object of his inquiry is *capital*, and not its surface categories (land, rent, wages, prices). The surface categories have a germ of truth in them, but they are only available in a 'stunted, or caricatured form.'

More was needed than the simple calculations of the accountants, who measured wages and raw materials, rents and energy charges to come up with the costs of production, and on the basis of this for their employers, the capitalists, to calibrate prices that would stand up as reasonable in the marketplace. Was profit simply the quantum between the market price (a function of demand and supply) and the costs of production? If that was the case, then what is the difference between the economic function in pre-capitalist times and under capitalism? Wouldn't feudal lords also make their profits based on such an elementary formula?

Marx's critique was not trans-historical (the examination of all categories that are trans-historical, he writes in *Grundrisse*, 'lies beyond political economy'). His political economy rested firmly on the soil of *bourgeois society*. His analysis turned on certain categories that were not universal, trans-historical abstractions. Labour, for instance, was not labour in general, labour of all time. It was labour in bourgeois society, labour that lives in a society where 'the notion of human equality has already acquired the fixity of a popular prejudice' (*Capital*, I, p. 65). Labour power is sold in the market, not labour (even though the profits of unfree labour, whether slavery or bondage, facilitated the down payment for the industrial revolution and continued to finance capital through the alchemy of accumulation by dispossession). It is through the magic of the manipulation of this labour power that Marx is able to demonstrate how surplus value emerges from the process of production; not through the anarchy of the market, but through the process of exploitation. *Concrete* labour, the work of a weaver or a tanner, has an impact on the use-value of a commodity. The weaver weaves cloth, whereas the tanner tans it. Both have a physical impact on the thing they produce. But this *concrete labour* is different from the *abstract social labour*, 'the expenditure of human labour-power or human labour in the abstract' (*Capital*, I, p. 78). It is customary, and erroneous to see the former (concrete labour) as bound by history (so that over the course of time, weavers do their weaving in different ways, with different mechanism), and the latter (abstract social labour) as trans-historical and universal (a category for all time). This distinction is not tenable. Better to see the various concrete labours as phenomenal forms of labour, and the abstract social labour as its essential form, not for all time, but in the era of the capitalist mode of production. Under capitalism, then, there are many kinds of concrete labours (writing a book, binding the book), but there is one overarching phenomenal form for labour, abstract social labour. The concept of abstract social labour provides Marx with the necessary means to determine his labour theory of value, as he does in the heart of *Capital* (Parts 3, 4 and 5).

The analysis is dazzling. It is not easy. Hegel's philosophical ideas (of essence and appearance) confront the dull concepts of political economy (of prices, rent, and interest), and these in turn run into the religious thought of the day (of fetishism and transubstantiation). Marx's method is reliant upon an equal acknowledgement of the various traditions, not only economics, but also philosophy. Otherwise one might read the entire discussion on the labour theory of value and find fault with it for something it does not claim to do (Marx was not only interested in *how* capitalism functioned. He remained transfixed by *what makes* capitalism function. This distinction was not apparent to people such as Vilfredo Pareto and the marginalists of our present time). I once had a discussion with a neo-classical economist who was outraged by the opening sections of *Capital.* I tried to explain to him that he missed the entire point of Marx's emphasis on the *objective illusions* of capitalism, with the 'money-name', as Marx puts it so deliciously, certainly an illusion, but one that must appear to us as the thing itself. This kind of philosophical consideration of the basic categories of *Capital* is essential, or else the book will have lost its power. Marx's work goes under the skin of the system. Marx was not only interested in the symptoms of capitalist crisis; he wanted to get to the root of the matter.

DRAFT PLANS

> Every movement in which the working class comes out *as a class* against the ruling classes and attempts to force them by pressure from without is a political movement. For instance, the attempt in a particular factory or even a particular industry to force a shorter working day out of the capitalists by strikes, etc., is a purely economic movement. On the other hand the movement to force an eight-hour day, etc., *law* is a *political* movement. And in this way, out of the separate economic movements of the workers there grows up everywhere a *political* movement, that is to say a movement of the *class*, with the object of achieving its interests in a general form, in a form possessing a general social force of compulsion.
> — Marx to Friedrich Bolte, November 23, 1871

Take courage. If it is hard to understand, it was hard enough for Marx to write. He recognized fairly early that his was not to be an analysis of a functional system, one that was absent the struggles of people to reshape the contradictions to their own ends. Capitalism was not a Swiss clock, which kept perfect time if well oiled. Inherent contradictions tore into the heart of the system. These could not be set aside (*ceteris paribus*). They were fundamental to his analysis. The problem was how to write about a dynamic system.

The research came handily. Marx then began to scribble from his research toward the mode of presentation. The various drafts can be seen in the *Grundrisse* and the *Theories of Surplus Value*. None of these had the ideal mode of presentation. In his afterword to the second edition (1873), Marx put it bluntly,

> Of course the method of presentation must differ in form from that of inquiry. The latter has to appropriate the material in detail, to analyze its different forms of development, to trace out their inner connection. Only after this work is done, can the actual movement be adequately described. If this is done successfully, if the life of the subject-matter is ideally reflected as in a mirror, then it may appear as if we had before us a mere a priori construction. (*Capital*, I, p. 28)

The book must open with the essence of the system. Initially Marx thought that this was capital. But it turned out that capital had to be broken down to its atomic structure, to the main atom, the commodity. In 1858, in the *Grundrisse*, Marx notes, 'The first category in which bourgeois wealth presents itself is that of the *commodity*.' At the level of the commodity, Marx was able to demonstrate the principle contradictions of the system. It was at the heart of critique.

The critique that begins at the level of the commodity is not simply to take us to the surface economic categories (price, rent, interest). Marx had a very detailed plan for his major work. The first three volumes, which we have in print, were to run from 'the phenomenon which constitute the *process of capitalist production as such* . . . with no regard for any of the secondary effects of outside influence' (Volume 1) to 'the *process of circulation*' (Volume 2) to 'the concrete forms which grow out of the *movements of capital as a whole*' (Volume 3).[3] This was one plan. Marx had about fourteen others. There is one from 1844 called the 'Draft Plan on The Modern State', which begins with a consideration of the French Revolution and ends with the abolition struggle. Later he produced very clear plans for his comprehensive system, of which two are illuminating. One from 1858 (letter to Engels, April 2):

1. *Volume on Capital.*
     a. Capital in general.
          i. Process of production of capital.
          ii. Process of circulation of capital.
          iii. Profit and interest.
     b.   On competition.
     c.   On credit.
     d.   On joint stock companies.
2. *Volume on Landed Property.*
3. *Volume on wage labour.*
4. *Volume on the State.*
5. *Volume on international trade.*
6. *Volume on the world market and crises.*

The other from 1866:

Volume 1: Process of production of capital.
Volume 2: Process of circulation of capital.
Volume 3: Forms of the process in its totality.
Volume 4: History of the theory.

It is clear from these plans that the work is not simply about economics. This is a theory of the capitalist mode of production, and of the bourgeois world order.

In 1848, Marx and Engels announced the centrality of class struggles. In this major work as well, class struggle plays a major role. In 1859 Marx published *A Contribution to the Critique of Political Economy*, the first draft of *Capital*. The book was little read. What is memorable about it is Marx's statement on history, where he notes that the economic base determines the social, political and cultural superstructure (the actual line is not so strong, with Marx simply saying, 'The mode of production of material life conditions the general process of social, political, and intellectual life', with the word *conditions* less imprisoning than *determines*). There is a cautionary note that Marx attaches to the next paragraph, which is often less cited. Here he says, 'In studying such transformations it is always necessary to distinguish between the material transformation of the economic conditions of production, which can be determined with the precision of natural science, and the legal, political, religious, artistic or philosophic – in short, ideological forms in which men become conscious of this conflict and fight it out.' The class struggle is an integral part of history. There is no evolution of economic forms. That much was clear to Marx when he first conjured up the proletariat as the agent of history in his *Economic and Philosophic Manuscripts* (written in 1844, when the German workers were barely out of their historical adolescence). The class struggle is everywhere in his mature works. In sections of *Capital,* one watches the capitalists in charge, as they rationalize production to create a process of accumulation in the factory system. In other parts, it is the workers who have the upper hand, as they use their concentration and their exploitation as the basis for political organization. The workers and the capitalists clash over who must have decisive control over the State, with all its trappings of neutrality. These glimpses of interest would have formed Marx's unfinished books on politics and international relations. He could not turn to it. It took him too long to revise the first few volumes, of which the twice-revised 1859 book was essentially a first draft.

In 1862, Marx wrote to Kugelmann with news that the new book, *the book,* would not bear the shopworn title, *Contribution to the Critique of Political Economy*, Part 2, but it 'will appear under the title *Capital,* with *A Contribution to the Critique of Political Economy* as merely the subtitle' (December 28, 1862). Having uncovered the centrality of the commodity, Marx could proceed. The opening chapters are hard he wrote in the preface ('beginnings are always difficult in all sciences'), but essential. Without a sense of his method, all would be lost. The book unfolds with forethought.

> Man's reflections on the forms of social life, and consequently, also, his scientific analysis of those forms, take a course directly opposite to that of their actual historical development. He begins, post festum, with the results of the process of development ready to hand before him. The characters that stamp products as commodities, and whose establishment is a necessary preliminary to the circulation of commodities, have already acquired the stability of natural, self-understood forms of social life, before man seeks to decipher, not their historical character, for in his eyes they are immutable, but their meaning. (*Capital,* I, p. 80)

'The presentation' of his book, he wrote in the preface, 'is improved'. He was right. It is.

NOTES

1 Heinz Frederick Peters, *Die Rote Jenny*. Published in English as *Red Jenny: A Life With Karl Marx*, 1987.
2 All references to *Capital* are from the LeftWord Books edition, New Delhi, 2010.
3 This is the plan Marx outlines in *Capital*, Volume III, p. 25.

Reading *Capital* in the Age of Finance

Jayati Ghosh

It is a big, unwieldy book in three fat volumes, with parts of it evidently incomplete. It was written nearly one and a half centuries ago, in a context that seems very different from our own. It aimed to describe the perceived economic and social reality of a particular time (the late nineteenth century) and place (northwest Europe). The writing is dense, even in the most accessible of the various English translations, with prolonged forays into tangential points and pedantic arguments with minor writers who are unknown today. In any case, the ideas are complex and certainly not easy to understand quickly.

So why read Karl Marx's *Capital* today? What insights can such a book provide to understanding current reality, in the form of a much more complex world that has become so much more globally integrated and technologically developed, of societies and economies that appear to be quite different from those of nineteenth-century England? Some would argue that that there is no point in ploughing through these massive tomes, that they are no longer really relevant or helpful to our understanding. But in fact, what is remarkable is the extent to which this massive work does still provide insights at so many different levels. More fundamentally, it continues to provide a useful framework for understanding the essential features of capitalism, no matter how varied its contemporary manifestations.

Consider only a few of these insights, which are particularly important in what can now be called the age of finance.

WHAT IS CAPITAL?

The central point about capital for Marx is that it is *not* just a resource in itself, a simple factor of production analogous to land and labour. Rather, it is an expression of very specific social relations of production, in particular historical contexts. This means that all means of production need not be capital. For example, a loom that is required to weave cloth is capital if it is used in a factory by a worker employed to produce cloth to be sold for profit, but it is not capital if it is used in a peasant household to create cloth to be used by the members of the household. The means of production become capital through the social relations that underlie the production process.

This is the social relation between employer and worker, which is what enables capitalist production to take place at all. This requires workers to be 'free' in a double sense. First, they must be 'free' to sell their own labour power, that is, not bound by other socio-economic ties and constraints that could prevent them working for wages and not be tied to any particular employer. Second, they must also necessarily be 'free' of any ownership of the means of production, so that they have no choice but to make themselves available for paid work for their own material survival. This makes labour power also a commodity, sold in the market for a value which is determined by social subsistence norms. The peculiar nature of this commodity is that those who sell it may appear to be (and in some respects are) free, but they live only as long as they find work, and they find work only as long as their labour serves capital.

Marx saw other forms of capital, such as usurer's capital and merchant capital, as 'antediluvian' forms of capital, which have existed as long as the history of money in many different types of society. They did not have the power to transform socio-economic relations, until they became fused with industrial capital. Marx himself did not treat finance capital separately, though later Marxists have explored the implications of the emergence of finance capital for the transformation of capitalism itself, through its association with the monopoly phase of capitalism and the strength of the financial oligarchy. But this does mean that using the term to encompass other forms – such as social capital, cultural capital and human capital – distorts Marx's notion, since this implicitly treats capital as a pure resource (however it is created) and assumes away the underlying social relations.

PRIMITIVE ACCUMULATION

The concentration of ownership of the means of production in a few hands is effectively what enables capital to play its role in production. But how does this concentration occur in the first place? It must obviously be based on the expropriation of the means of production from those who previously possessed it, such as peasants and small artisans who could have produced on their own. 'Free labourers, in the double sense that neither they themselves form part and parcel of the means of production, as in the case of slaves, bondsmen, &c., nor do the means of production belong to them, as in the case of peasant-proprietors; they are, therefore, free from, unencumbered by, any means of production of their own' (*Capital*, I, p. 668).[1]

Marx points out that historically such expropriation (the primitive accumulation of capital) has been a violent process, emphasising the forcible creation of the 'double freedom' of labour. 'The historical movement which changes the producers into wage-workers, appears, on the one hand, as their emancipation from serfdom and from the fetters of the guilds, and this side alone exists for our bourgeois historians. But, on the other hand, these new freedmen became sellers of themselves only after they had been robbed of all their own means of production, and of all the guarantees of existence afforded by the old feudal arrangements. . . . The history of this, their expropriation, is written in the annals of mankind in letters of blood and fire' (*Capital*, I, p. 669). Capitalist production and capitalist private property 'have for their fundamental condition the annihilation of self-earned private property; in other words, the expropriation of the labourer' (*Capital*, I, p. 724).

Because of uneven development, primitive accumulation is not simply a historical fact but a continuing reality, which is constantly being experienced especially in the developing world today.

COMMODITY FETISHISM

Unlike feudal extraction of surplus, capital operates on a purely contractual economic basis, through the voluntary market exchange of goods and commodities. But even this, while it seems as the outcome of rational choices of individuals, actually relies on a widespread social illusion. Marx calls this 'commodity fetishism' — the situation in which relations between people become mediated by relations between things, commodities and money.

Commodities are not simply things or objects, because they contain two very specific and different features, that is they possess both use value (meeting human needs or wants) and exchange value (as a thing that can be traded in return for something else). The two features may bear no relation to one another, and the process of exchange and the determination of exchange value are determined not by features intrinsic to the commodity but external to it. However, the contradictory nature of commodities gives rise to the possibility — indeed likelihood — that its varying features are confused and conflated. Commodity fetishism occurs when value is seen as intrinsic to commodities rather than being the result of labour, and the exchange of commodities and market-based interaction are seen as the 'natural' way of dealing with all objects, rather than as a historically specific set of social relations.

More broadly, commodity fetishism is the illusion emerging from the centrality of private property in capitalism, which then determines not only how people work and interact, but even how they perceive reality and understand social change. The urge to acquisition, the obsession with material gratification of wants and the ordering of human well-being in terms of their ability to command different commodities, could all be described as forms of commodity fetishism. So too could socio-economic analyses that mistake the commodity illusion for genuine material and human conditions.

THE DYNAMISM OF CAPITAL

The nature of capital is constantly to transform itself and the society in which it operates. As Marx put it in the *Communist Manifesto*: 'The bourgeoisie cannot exist without constantly revolutionising the instruments of production, and thereby the relations of production, and with them the whole relations of society. . . . Constant revolutionizing of production, uninterrupted disturbance of all social conditions, everlasting uncertainty and agitation distinguish the bourgeois epoch from all earlier ones. All fixed, fast frozen relations, with their train of ancient and venerable prejudices and opinions, are swept away, all new-formed ones become antiquated before they can ossify. All that is solid melts into air . . .'[2]

This dynamism of capital has many unprecedented and positive results: a cosmopolitan character of production, which is particularly evident in the current phase of globalization; rapid improvements in technology and the creation of 'colossal' productive forces; immensely facilitated means of communication; the agglomeration of populations into cities; much greater interaction and interdependence of nations not only in economic terms but also in intellectual and creative life. Capital generates new types of production organization and economic institutions: not just the factory system but more recent arrangements, financial institutions and structures, legal systems. This constant revolutionising of production processes and institutions is evident even today, especially in the emergence of finance capital.

Marx identified three 'cardinal facts' of capitalist production: (*i*) Concentration of means of production in a few hands, whereby they cease to appear as the property of the immediate labourers and turn into social production capacities; (*ii*) The organization of labour into social labour: through co-operation, division of labour and the uniting of labour with the natural sciences; and (*iii*) the creation of the world market. This third feature is the natural result of the tendency of the system to spread and aggrandise itself, to destroy and incorporate earlier forms of production, and to transform technology and institutions constantly. Yet the globalization also occurs in the form of uneven development, which is then expressed spatially and regionally as well as within particular areas. Further, this creation of a world market in turn creates its own problems, as Marxists like Rosa Luxemburg and Prabhat Patnaik have identified: it progressively reduces the ability of capitalism to prey upon pre-capitalist or non-capitalist systems, which underlies the ability of the system to expand.

THE ROLE OF CREDIT

When Marx was writing, finance was mainly confined to banking, to the provision of credit by banks that were newly emerging as 'modern' banks. The incredible proliferation and sophistication of financial markets, that allow risk to be disguised in various ways and prevent attempts at public control, had not yet emerged. Even so, Marx perceptively noted the implications of the provision of credit both in developing capitalism's productive capacity and in making it more prone to crises. Thus he agued: 'The credit system appears as the main lever of over-production and over-speculation in commerce solely because the reproduction process, which is elastic by nature, is here forced to its extreme limits, and is so forced because a large part of the social capital is employed by people who do not own it and who consequently tackle things quite differently than the owner, who anxiously weighs the limitations of his private capital in so far as he handles it himself. . . . Hence, the credit system accelerates the material development of the productive forces and the development of the world market. . . . At the same time credit accelerates the violent eruptions of this contradiction — crises — and thereby the elements of disintegration of the old mode of production of the old mode of production' (*Capital*, III, p. 441).

Marx also noted the role of 'fictitious capital', which he saw as the inevitable result of interest-bearing capital. This he described as the paper claim to the ownership of capital that exists in a form that is independent of the actual material capital, and can be traded in financial markets. While the growth of such fictitious capital can additionally help to mobilize resources for real capital accumulation, because of the possibility of its autonomous expansion, it can also trigger and amplify crises. Such an argument can be extended to understand the boom-and-bust tendencies of credit and financial markets that have been elaborated by Charles Kindleberger, Hyman Minsky and Jan Kregel.

This perception also allowed Marx to note how financial fraud becomes an integral part of the system, and in turn allows for the continued economic differentiation upon which the entire system rests. 'The two characteristics of the credit system are, on the one hand, to develop the incentive of capitalist production, enrichment through the exploitation of the labour of others, to the purest and most colossal form of gambling and swindling, and to reduce more and more the number of the few who exploit the social wealth; and on the other hand, to constitute the form of transition to a new mode of production. It is this ambiguous nature which endows the principal spokesmen of credit . . . with the pleasant character mixture of swindler and prophet' (*Capital*, III, p. 441).

CONCENTRATION OF CAPITAL AND UNEVEN DEVELOPMENT

The accumulation of capital generates higher productivity and transforms systems, but it is also associated with uneven development. A central feature is the centralization of capital, which expresses the inherent antagonism between capitals: 'Accumulation, therefore, presents itself as increasing concentration of the means of production, and of the command over labour; on the other, as repulsion of many individual capitals from one another. . . . It is concentration of capitals already formed, destruction of their individual independence, expropriation of capitalist by capitalist, transformation of many small into few large capitals. . . . Capital grows in one place to a huge mass in a single hand, because it has in another place been lost by many' (*Capital*, I, p. 586).

Marx saw capitalism as being in a state of continuous disequilibrium, because of the tendency of uneven development. This is not confined to a single arena, but rather characterises all of the social and economic relations that develop under capitalism. Thus, there is an inherent tendency for the expansion of the productive forces and the ability of the economic system to generate sufficient demand for the goods that are produced, which can give rise to 'realization crises'. There is disproportionality between the expansion of fixed and variable capital, which generates the rising organic composition of capital that for Marx makes it more difficult to generate profits. There is the disproportionality between sectors that emerges in the process of accumulation. There is the geographical aspect of uneven development, which emerges from the tendency of capital to concentrate and creates at once both 'developed' and 'underdeveloped' areas. And of course, there is the lack of congruence between money as a medium of exchange and money as a measure of value, which tends to be amplified by the development of credit and the expansion of the financial system, which in turn creates a tendency to crisis.

CONFLICT, CONTRADICTIONS AND CRISES

Obviously, Marx saw capitalism as having an inherent and continuous tendency to experience crises. But there are many levels of conflict and contradiction that occur because of the system, and only some of them culminate in periodic crises that mark capitalist expansion. Since the basic dynamics of capital is simultaneously to aggrandise itself and impoverish other classes such as workers and peasants, within and across nations, it obviously generates class conflicts. Marx saw these as essential and continuous elements of social and material life under capitalism. But the system also generates intra-class conflict, pitting individual capital against other capitals and the individual worker against other workers. There is a Darwinian struggle for survival constantly at work, so individualism, conflict and competition become the driving forces of the system.

At the same time, individualism and competition between capitals also create what Marx calls the anarchy of the market and the inevitable tendency towards crises. Overproduction in terms of the market (even when human needs of all the people in the society need not be satisfied) is a characteristic feature simply because of the way individual capitals operate in the drive to generate more profit. As a result, the process of accumulation is never smooth. Rather, it is uneven and punctuated by crises. Partly, this is the result of the very success of capitalism in delivering more economic growth and technological advance. 'The stupendous productivity developing under the capitalist mode of production relative to population, and the increase (not just of their material substance) which grows much more rapidly than the population, contradict the basis, which constantly narrows in relation to the existing wealth, and for which all this immense productiveness works. They also contradict the conditions under which this swelling capital augments its value. Hence the crisis' (*Capital*, III, p. 266).

These periodic crises are a way of resolving the contradictions inherent in the dynamics of capitalism, albeit in a sharp and possibly violent way. Because the underlying imbalance is typically one of overproduction (relative to demand, not need) such crises usually involve the destruction of a significant proportion of existing products and productive forces. Marx described the workings of one particular form of crisis, resulting from price deflation, as follows: 'definite presupposed price relations govern the process of reproduction, so that the latter is halted and thrown into confusion by a general drop in prices. This confusion and stagnation paralyzes the function of money as a medium of payment, whose development is geared to the development of capital and is based on those presupposed price relations. The chain of payment obligations due at specific dates is broken in a hundred places. The confusion is augmented by the attendant collapse of the credit system, which develops simultaneously with capital, and leads to violent and acute crises, sudden forcible depreciations to the actual stagnation and disruption of the process of reproduction, and thus to a real falling off in reproduction' (*Capital*, III, p. 254).

It is important to note that for Marx, crises under capitalism are never purely 'financial' or 'monetary' — rather they reflect the real imbalances, disproportionalities and uneven development that are fundamental features of capitalist accumulation. So what is actually the result of the uneven development of the forces of production appears as a crisis of exchange or (in contemporary terms) finance.

THE DOMINANCE OF FINANCE CAPITAL

Marx was writing in the era of industrial capital, although the preliminary signs of the concentration and centralization of production were already evident and allowed him to interpret these as indications of the likely future tendency of the system. However, the rise to dominance of finance, which has really occurred over the past century (and has got accentuated in the past thirty years) has other implications, which can even be said to have transformed the nature of capitalism. It is both a consequence of and a contributor to the larger process of national and international concentration and centralization of production. Lenin described the era of finance capital as the last stage of capitalism, characterized not only by extreme concentration of capital but heightened imperialistic tendencies expressed in the struggle of large capital for the control of *economic* (not necessarily geographic) territory.

What exactly does the dominance of finance entail? To begin with, it has accelerated and intensified the process of making capitalism the international system *par excellence*. The process of globalisation, which can be said to be the defining feature of the era of finance capital, involves not only greater trade integration but also the mobility of finance across borders. Thus centralization of national capitals has been intertwined with, and even dominated by, the centralization of multinational capital through the process of globalization. This in turn means, as Prabhat Patnaik has elaborated, that finance capital is no longer particularly 'national', that there is no coalescence of the interests of industrial and finance capital as was described by Lenin, and that inter-imperialist rivalries tend to be subsumed by the global requirements of mobile finance.[3]

The dominance of finance has inevitably increased the fragility of the economic system and the tendency to periodic crises, since financial over-accumulation can occur and cause volatility even when the real economy does not show the tendency to the same degree, as C.P. Chandrasekhar has elaborated.[4]

The growing power of global finance capital can in turn be seen as part of a wide political economy process, a result of the attempt in developed capitalism to use the expansion of finance (which some call 'financialization'[5]) to counter the inherent tendencies towards stagnation in mature capitalism. But such a process is counter-productive, since in addition to increasing the proclivity to periodic crises, the concentration of finance capital also contributes to overall stagnationary tendencies in the manner outlined by Patnaik.[6]

There are several ways in which this occurs. One crucial mechanism is that internationally mobile finance constrains the ability of nation states to engage in demand management policies that would reduce or mitigate slumps. Financial markets can punish most effectively any economic policies they do not like, by causing capital flight that creates external and internal economic crises. So governments find it much more difficult to intervene to shore up domestic demand or to put in place policies that would lead to more egalitarian distribution of income and assets. Since mobile finance capital is perceived by governments to abhor fiscal deficits and resent higher rates of taxation, it effectively constrains public expenditure. It inhibits governments from undertaking expenditures that could directly and indirectly increase employment and economic activity in the system as a whole.

It is therefore no accident that the period of the rise to dominance of finance is also the period of the hegemony of neo-liberal ideology in determining economic policies. Economic neoliberalism does not actually imply a withdrawal of the state from economic activity, as many tend to assume: rather it implies a shift in the nature of state involvement, away from attempting to provide social and economic rights of citizens, to ensuring conditions of profitability for large capital and in particular finance. Thus, even though the hegemony of finance is associated with even greater instability and economic injustice, its political power and ability to affect state policies tends to be largely unconstrained, as the current global crisis shows. Increasingly, this is true of economies at very different levels of development.

SOCIAL REPRODUCTION

One aspect of the economy that was generally neglected in Marx's *Capital*, but is still critical to understanding the dynamics of capitalism, is the role of unpaid labour, especially in social reproduction. Marx's major insight was to show that the worker receives the value of her/his labour power, but produces a greater value through labour, the difference being the surplus value accruing to the employer. But what he did not recognize is that the value of labour power is effectively underwritten by the unpaid labour involved in social reproduction, usually within the household. Work by Diane Elson[7] and Nancy Folbre[8] has shown how critical this is in maintaining structures of capitalism and shaping their development. The capitalist economy can be sub-divided into the 'commodity economy', characterized by financial and market transactions, and the 'care' economy characterized by output that is not sold in the market and unpaid labour. The typical gender construction of societies usually allocates the greater part of this unpaid labour that is essential for social reproduction to women, even though such unpaid labour need not be exclusive to women. The interaction between these two economies is an important underlying feature of the dynamics of capitalism, which remains inadequately studied.

THE ATTITUDE TO NATURE

Another aspect of the economy which was not given too much explicit attention in Marx's *Capital* is the relationship of the economic system with the natural environment. But the framework provided in it does allow us to extend the analysis to this crucial area. Production inevitably involves the interaction of human beings with nature, but this interaction is determined by the social organization of production. The capitalist system subsumes the richness and complexity of nature into the simplistic category 'natural resources' and insists on their conversion into commodities, which can be priced and exchanged. This is not only philosophically limiting and socially unjust, it is also deeply dangerous for the eventual sustainability of the system itself because it leads to rapacious extraction and degradation. Thus, even when capitalism is able to reform and restructure itself periodically (whether through crises or through state intervention) it cannot effectively deal with the ecological crises provoked by its own expansion. Environmental problems then emerge as the result of a social system spinning out of control, which also has global distributional implications. As John Bellamy Foster has argued, 'Capital . . . is running up against ecological barriers at a biospheric level that cannot be overcome, as was the case previously, through the "spatial fix" of geographical expansion and exploitation. Ecological imperialism – the growth of the centre of the system at unsustainable rates, through the more thorough-going ecological degradation of the periphery – is now generating a planetary-scale set of ecological contradictions, imperilling the entire biosphere.'[9]

ALIENATION

A fundamental feature of the capitalist system that Marx described, and one that has complex social and philosophical underpinnings, is alienation. Once again, this is different from the term as commonly understood – an individual person's feeling of estrangement from society or community. The Marxian concept of alienation is more systemic, and refers to not an isolated experience, but to a generalized state of the broad mass of subjects. So it expresses not the personal experience of an individual worker, but rather the very nature of wage labour, which is the central social relationship in capitalism. Most simply put, it can be expressed as the loss of control by workers over their own work. This alienation of the workers means that they effectively cease to be autonomous human beings, because they cannot control their workplace, the products they produce, or even the way they relate to each other. Because this fundamentally defines their conditions of existence, this means that workers can never become autonomous and self-realised human and social beings under capitalism.

Such alienation combines with commodity fetishism to create a peculiar kind of unfreedom of workers, within a perceived social and material context in which they are apparently free. Istvan Meszaros has noted that the so-called individual emancipation that is brought about by the bourgeois revolution is really nothing more than the creation of 'universal saleability', so that every living creature is effectively transformed into property.[10] As Meszaros puts it: 'Alienation is therefore characterized by the universal extension of "saleability"; by the conversion of human beings into "things" so that they could appear as commodities on the market; and by the fragmentation of the social body into "isolated individuals" who pursued their own limited, particularistic aims "in servitude to egoistic need", making a virtue out of their selfishness in their cult of privacy.'

Obviously, genuine social emancipation therefore becomes impossible in such a system. That is why revolutionary change for socialism was the essential goal in all of Marx's writings. Of course, the question of what are the essential features of socialism is a much more complex question, which has been subject to very diverse interpretations in both theory and practice over the past one and half centuries. With the benefit of historical experience in the period since *Capital* was written, it may be possible to conclude that such socialist revolution must be seen not as a moment, but as a process.

NOTES

1 All references to *Capital* are from the LeftWord Books edition, New Delhi, 2010.

2 The text of the *Manifesto* is reproduced in *A World to Win: Essays on the Communist Manifesto*, edited by Prakash Karat, New Delhi: LeftWord, 1999. This quotation appears on p. 92.

3 'Introduction' to Lenin's *Imperialism, the Highest Stage of Capitalism*, New Delhi: LeftWord, 2000.

4 C.P. Chandrasekhar, 'Financial Liberalization, Fragility and the Socialization of Risk', *G24 Discussion Papers*, 2004, available at www.g24.org/002gva04.pdf.

5 Gerald Epstein (ed.), *Financialization and the World Economy*, Edward Elgar, 2005.

6 'Introduction' to Lenin's *Imperialism*.

7 Diane Elson, *Male Bias in the Development Process*, Manchester University Press, 1995.

8 Nancy Folbre, *The Invisible Heart: Economics and Family Values*, New York: The New Press, 2001.

9 John Bellamy Foster, *The Ecological Revolution: Making Peace with the Planet*, New York: Monthly Review Press, 2009, p. 249.

10 Istvan Meszaros, *Marx's Theory of Alienation*, Cambridge University Press, 1970.

Agriculture and Rural Society in *Capital*

R. Ramakumar

This essay is intended to introduce the reader to the treatment of agriculture in the three volumes of *Capital*.[1] Marx's *Capital* is a work on the capitalist mode of production in its totality, and not a sector-wise analysis of a capitalist economy. There are no chapters that deal exclusively with agriculture. As historical change in societies is central to Marx's treatment of capitalism, every chapter has references to the changes that take place in agriculture. Yet, one could try and delineate certain features of change in agriculture that are discussed across the three volumes. They are,

(a) the idea of primitive accumulation;
(b) the nature of pre-capitalist relationships; and
(c) the idea of rent in agriculture.

The discussion under the above three heads is in no way exhaustive. Further, there are considerable overlaps of ideas and concepts across the three heads. However, this essay has a limited role of introducing the discussion, rather than explaining themes in their detail.

PRIMITIVE ACCUMULATION AND DOUBLE FREEDOM

Labour Power as a Commodity
For Marx, the starting point of the analysis of capitalist mode of production is 'commodity production'. The existence of commodities is not a phenomenon specific to capitalism. Even under a pre-capitalist mode of production, a large number of products of human labour were exchanged in the market. However, the commodification of the *labour power* of labourers is the most distinguishing feature of capitalism. The labourer sells his labour power to the capitalist. The capitalist buys it, uses it to produce new commodities and sells them to make a profit out of it. The historical

uniqueness of labour power as a commodity comes from the fact that it is at once an *embodiment* of use-values as also a *source* of use-values (*Capital*, I, Ch. 6).

The commodification of labour power constitutes a turning point in the history of mankind. In pre-capitalist modes of production, labourers were neither free nor obliged to offer their labour power as a commodity, as they were either slaves or serfs or labourers, bonded in a variety of ways. Marx distinguishes the slave (who himself was a commodity) from the serf (who parts with only a part of his labour power) and the wage worker (whose labour power was fully commoditised). *Primitive accumulation*

In many pre-capitalist societies, the completion of the process of commodification of labour power faces a central obstacle.[2] The prospective sellers of labour power are also possessors of means of production i.e., land. As a result, a large section of the rural population is in a position to produce and sell commodities into which their own labour was incorporated. In such a circumstance, according to Marx, the owners of *money* are unable to transform it into *capital*. In order to transform money into capital, the owner of money must meet in the market with the labourer, who is *obliged* to offer his labour power for sale as a commodity. Such obligation can be achieved only by forcefully separating the labourer from his means of production.

For Marx, *primitive accumulation* is the process of separation of the labourer from his means of production, leaving with him nothing but his labour power. By definition, primitive accumulation *precedes* capital accumulation; it forms the *historic basis* of a specifically capitalist production; it *clears the way* for a capitalist system to stand on its own legs. In an important formulation, Marx writes that

> ... the accumulation of capital pre-supposes surplus-value; surplus-value pre-supposes capitalistic production; capitalistic production presupposes the pre-existence of considerable masses of capital and of labour power in the hands of producers of commodities. The whole movement, therefore, seems to turn in a vicious circle, out of which we can only get by supposing a primitive accumulation ... preceding capitalistic accumulation; an accumulation not the result of the capitalistic mode of production, but its starting point. (*Capital*, I, p. 667)[3]

The Duality of Freedom

The major feature of primitive accumulation of capital is the appearance of 'free labourers, in the double sense'. First, the immediate producer ceases to be a slave, serf, or bonded labourer as in the pre-capitalist era. Instead, he becomes the 'untrammelled owner of his capacity for labour, i.e., *of his person*' (*Capital*, I, p. 165). Secondly, however, immediate producers also become 'free from, unencumbered by, any means of production of their own' (V-I, p. 714). The old patron-client relationship breaks down, and the labourer is totally left to himself. In Marx's own words,

> ... the historical movement which changes the producers into wage-workers, appears, on the one hand, as their emancipation from serfdom and from the fetters of the guilds, and *this side alone exists for our bourgeois historians*. But, on the other hand, these new freedmen became sellers of themselves only after they had been robbed of all their own means of production, and of all the guarantees of existence afforded by the old feudal arrangements. (*Capital*, I, p. 669; emphasis added.)

The dual nature of change under primitive accumulation is central to any understanding of capitalism in a historical sense, even in the contemporary age of imperialism. Non-Marxist writers have everywhere failed to appreciate the significance of Marx's concept of double freedom. Bourgeois social scientists herald the stage of primitive accumulation, and capitalism, as the embodiment of human freedoms. However, they fail to see that the capitalist would not have been in a position to corner profits for himself in the absence of the historical appearance of a class, which was left with the sale of its labour power as the only means of livelihood.

On the other hand, many strands of post-structuralist writings emphasise only the second component of the change. Capitalism is not a meaningful historical category for post-structuralist writers, and they inaccurately replace it with the vague term 'development'. For them, the modern era is marked by 'development-induced violence' that is continuously dislocating 'local communities' that have 'lived with nature' in 'loving interaction with Mother Earth' for thousands of years (see Mies and Shiva, 1993; Kothari and Harcourt, 2004). Such descriptions are, of course, objectively incorrect. But more importantly, these descriptions have a one-sided and ahistorical understanding of the *totality* of changes in individual freedoms that Marx wrote about. Post-structuralist writers romanticise pre-capitalist social structures and pass over what David Harvey (2007) terms as the 'repressive intimacy' of traditional communities.

The 'freedom' that capitalism provides to the labourer during the transition from forms of bonded labour to wage labour has been central to the debates on agrarian change. Unlike neo-classical or libertarian writings, which emphasise only on the *negative freedoms* of workers, Marxist writers use a wider and richer conception of *positive freedoms* and emphasise on the freedom of self-determination of workers (see Rao, 1999 for a review). In a study on the transition of unfree labourers to free labourers in a south Indian village, Ramachandran (1990) writes:

> Marx distinguishes between (to use the term used by Jon Elster) the *formal freedom* of the worker under capitalism and the *real unfreedom* of workers in pre-capitalist systems: 'the freedom of workers to change employers makes him free in a way not found in earlier modes of production' . . . The extension of the freedom of workers in a society to sell their labour power is an enhancement of their positive freedom, which is, in turn, an important measure of how well that society is doing.[4]

Marx, in *Capital*, I, Chapter 6, describes the concept of 'formal freedom' with great clarity. Concluding a discussion on labour power, he guides the reader from the sphere of *circulation*, where the exchange of labour power takes place, to the 'hidden abode of *production*', where the consumption of labour power is completed.

> This sphere that we are deserting, within whose boundaries the sale and purchase of labour-power goes on, is in fact a very Eden of the innate rights of man. There alone rule Freedom, Equality, Property and Bentham. Freedom, because both buyer and seller of a commodity . . . are constrained only by their own free will. They contract as free agents, and the agreement they come to, is but the form in which they give legal expression to their common will. Equality, because each enters into relation with the other, as with a simple owner of commodities, and they exchange equivalent for equivalent. Property, because each disposes only of what is his own. And Bentham, because each looks only to himself. The only force that brings them together

and puts them in relation with each other is the selfishness, the gain and the private interests of each . . .

. . . On leaving this sphere of simple circulation or of exchange of commodities, . . . we can perceive a change in the physiognomy of our *dramatis personae*. He, who before was the money-owner, now strides in front as capitalist; the possessor of labour-power follows as his labourer. The one with an air of importance, smirking, intent on business; the other, timid and holding back, like one who is bringing his own hide to market and has nothing to expect but — a hiding. (*Capital*, I, p. 172)

After presenting the conceptual framework of primitive accumulation, Marx goes on to describe the ways in which primitive accumulation proceeded in England between the 12th and 18th centuries, culminating in the entrenchment of the capitalist mode of production by the 19th century (see Chapters 27 to 30 in Volume I). These chapters also represent a summary history of agrarian capitalism in England — what Marx called the 'agricultural revolution'. The discussion of the English path in Marx forms the theoretical starting point for the study of paths of agrarian transition in other societies.

AGRICULTURAL REVOLUTION IN ENGLAND

The Expropriation of the Agricultural Population
England in the beginning of the 15th century was marked by the presence of 'free peasant proprietors'. Serfdom had ended by the last decade of the 14th century. However, a 'special class' of agricultural labourers had not yet formed. Smaller peasant proprietors supplemented their income by working for wages in the fields of others. They also benefited substantially from access to common lands, where they could graze cattle and collect forest resources.

The formation of a class of proletarians, free in the double sense, was achieved primarily by expropriating free peasant proprietors from their land. A number of processes played a role in this expropriation. First, a large number of 'feudal retainers', who possessed small plots of land attached to large manors, were evicted from their land in the 15th and 16th centuries.

Secondly, the Protestant Reformation of the 16th century gave a boost to the break up of estates of the Church. On the one hand, the dissolution of monasteries attached to the Church converted its labouring population into proletarians. On the other, large areas of Church land were given away to a few royal favourites and speculating farmers, who evicted tenants attached to those lands in large numbers.

Thirdly, the most important push to the expropriation came from the Enclosure Movement. The enclosure movement represented a successful effort by the landed interests to usurp the common lands accessed by peasants and convert them into private property. While the conversion of common lands into private lands had been a continuing process in England from the 16th century, its character qualitatively changed by the 18th century; given the change in the nature of the state itself, enclosures came to be carried out with legal sanction. The use of legal means to usurp common lands was a reflection of the continuing influence of the landowning class in the then Parliament.

Eric Hobsbawm (1968) has written about two different kinds of impacts that enclosures had. On the one hand, it brought previously uncultivated land into cultivation and allowed enterprising landowners to improve cultivation with new investments. On the other hand, it displaced large numbers of small landholders from land and added them to the burgeoning wage labour force. According to Maurice Dobb (1963), in the presence of continuous agricultural improvements, expropriation of lands may also have, additionally, taken place 'without any explicit act of eviction'. He writes:

> In addition to forcible eviction, many small holders, burdened by debt or in the later eighteenth and early nineteenth century cut off from their traditional by-employments in cottage industry or adversely affected by the growing competition of larger farms equipped with newer agricultural methods, requiring capital, must have surrendered their holdings to the more well-to-do peasant or to some improving landlord without any explicit act of eviction. (Dobb, 1963, p. 227)

Legislation Against the Expropriated

The reaction of the bourgeoisie to the rising numbers of the proletariat was more brutal than the act of expropriation itself. The large numbers of free members of the proletariat could not be fully absorbed into the nascent manufacturing sector. Unable to adapt to the disciplines of the new world, these labourers turned into 'beggars, robbers [and] vagabonds, partly from inclination, in most cases from stress of circumstances' (*Capital*, I, p. 686). The ruling class responded with the 'bloody legislation against vagabondage', which stamped vagabonds as criminals.

The logic of primitive accumulation is such that the bourgeoisie requires and uses the power of the state to compress wages, lengthen the working day and thwart resistance. For Marx, 'this is an essential element of the so-called primitive accumulation' (*Capital*, I, p. 689).[5] The laws enacted were not simply inhuman in an ethical sense; they were an attempt to transform the newly formed free and asset-less class into a usable labour force that would conform to the disciplines of a wage system. Employers were prohibited from paying wages higher than in the statute, and taking wages higher than in the statute invited severe punishment. Trade unions and other forms of labour coalitions were banned and 'treated as a heinous crime' (*Capital*, I, p. 690).

Over time, as capital accumulation proceeds, the need for compulsion in the disciplining of the proletariat receded. This was because the constancy of pressure under the capitalist mode of production — what Marx calls the 'dull compulsion of economic relations' — made the subjection of the labourer to the capitalist appear to be complete and natural. Direct force came to be used only exceptionally. He notes:

> The advance of capitalist production develops a working-class, which by education, tradition, habit, looks upon the conditions of that mode of production as self-evident laws of Nature. The organisation of the capitalist process of production, once fully developed, breaks down all resistance. The constant generation of a relative surplus-population keeps the law of supply and demand of labour, and therefore keeps wages, in a rut that corresponds with the wants of capital. (*Capital*, I, p. 689)

The Genesis of the Capitalist Farmer

The class of capitalist farmers in England was drawn primarily from the groups that were able to consolidate large holdings as private property between the 15th and 17th centuries. Marx writes that in the second half of the 14th century, the serf was transformed into a 'farmer', who received seed, cattle and implements from the landlord, paid a rent and employed moderate amounts of wage labour. It was by the end of the 16th century that the capitalist farmer appeared on the scene, who invested his own capital, employed large number of wage labourers, generated a surplus value and paid a part of the surplus value as rent to the landlord. As Hobsbawm and Rude (1973) have noted, this was the 'triple division into landlords, tenant farmers and hired labourers' that marked English agrarian capitalism.

Economic historians have argued that the capitalist farmer evolved from a long drawn-out process of differentiation of the peasantry, a process termed as 'capitalism from below'. In other words, the capitalist tenants were drawn from the ranks of the upper peasantry and artisanal masters, who had some base in the urban areas (Dobb, 1963; Brenner, 1976).

As Hobsbawm (1962) has noted, agrarian capitalism in England was accompanied by increases in agricultural production and productivity, which contributed to the industrial revolution; agricultural growth eased the wage goods constraint by feeding the rapidly rising non-agricultural population.

Creation of the Home-Market

One of the most important ways in which primitive accumulation contributed to the industrial revolution in the 18th and 19th centuries was through the expansion of the home market. The very process of expropriation of the working people in town and country in the transition to capitalism led also to the creation of an expanding home market. As Lenin was to write, 'the rural proletarian, by comparison with the middle peasantry, consumes less . . . *but buys more*' (Lenin, 1964b, p. 184). When household-based production units of artisans and smaller peasants continued to be active, they did so by serving groups of scattered customers across the countryside and towns. This mode of marketing was a major barrier to the creation of the 'one great market' that lumpy industrial capital required.

Primitive accumulation breaks down the unity between agriculture and industry in rural areas, as it contributes to the creation of a home market for industrial capital. But Marx is quick to qualify this statement; he says that even an exhaustive process of primitive accumulation does not uproot either small-scale farming or artisanal groups. That remains the task of modern industry.

> Modern Industry alone, and finally, supplies, in machinery, the lasting basis of capitalistic agriculture, expropriates radically the enormous majority of the agricultural population, and completes the separation between agriculture and rural domestic industry, whose roots — spinning and weaving — it tears up. It therefore also, for the first time, conquers for industrial capital the entire home-market. (*Capital*, I, pp. 700–01)

Colonialism and Primitive Accumulation

As Habib (1995) has noted, primitive accumulation in England rested on two pillars: 'internal exploitation,' which included the expropriation of the peasantry; and 'external plunder,' which was linked to global colonial dominance. According to Habib, a number of British historians have been rather indifferent to the importance of colonialism in aiding the process of industrial accumulation in England. In Chapters 31 and 33 of Volume I, Marx undertakes a brief analysis of colonialism. He notes:

> The discovery of gold and silver in America, the extirpation, enslavement and entombment in mines of the aboriginal population, the beginning of the conquest and looting of the East Indies, the turning of Africa into a warren for the commercial hunting of black skins, signalised the rosy dawn of the era of capitalist production. *These idyllic proceedings are the chief momenta of primitive accumulation.* (*Capital,* I, pp. 703)

Marx specifically noted the role played by the English East India Company in the transfer of resources to England, through monopolising trade between England and India as well as within India, and that it gave a significant push to English industrialisation. After 1757, first through the Company and then the Crown itself, large amounts of tributary payments were transferred from India to England. The tributes were remitted mainly through the export of textiles in the first phase and commercial crops in the later phase. According to one estimate, the Indian tribute to England in the 1780s amounted to an annual average of about £ 4.93 million (Habib, 2006). England, thus, typically ran huge trade deficits with India. According to Patnaik (2006), if we consider England's trade deficits with the West Indies and India alone, total investment in England could be raised by between two-thirds to over four-fifths in the period between 1770 and 1820. Thus, says Marx, 'primitive accumulation went on without the advance of a shilling' (*Capital,* I, pp. 704).[6]

Variations from the English Path

The essential question in the study of paths of agrarian transition in different societies is whether and how a class of agricultural labourers was formed, through primitive accumulation, out of the pre-capitalist cultivating groups. Experiences of transition in continental Western Europe, as well as in North

America and Asia, were quite different from that of England. Marxist scholars have always been careful to understand these variations in the paths of transition in societies outside England (for a review, see Byres, 1986). One of the first to caution against a schematic understanding of Marx's treatment of England was Lenin. He noted that:

> ... infinitely diverse combinations of elements of this or that type of capitalist evolution are possible, and only hopeless pedants could set about solving the peculiar and complex problems arising merely by quoting this or that opinion of Marx about a different historical epoch. (Lenin, 1964b, p. 33)

Lenin (1977) himself pointed out that there could be two forms of capitalist transition open to Russia. The first was the *Prussian path*, where a feudal landlord economy dominated by Junkers was not smashed completely, but reformed slowly to transform into a bourgeois economy. Lenin was not a votary of the Junker path because it retained elements of the feudal society for a long time without dissolving them. On the other hand, Lenin was more enthusiastic about what he called the *American path*. Here, as illustrated by the experience of North America, either there are no landlords historically, or the landlords are eliminated by confiscating and splitting up their feudal estates. The outcome of this path is that 'the peasant predominates, becomes the sole agent of agriculture, and evolves into a capitalist farmer'.[7]

In Asia, the paths of transition in Japan, South Korea and Taiwan have also been vastly different. In Japan, even though feudalism was weakened after the Meiji Restoration in 1868, a complete overthrow of landlords occurred only after the Second World War. After 1945, the occupant American military implemented land reform to politically weaken the hostile Japanese landlord class. Land reform contributed significantly to capitalist industrialisation in Japan, though the beginnings of industrialisation were in the Meiji period, when landlords were slowly turning capitalist farmers (Dore, 1959).

In South Korea and Taiwan too, it was the American military that implemented land reform after 1949 (Ahmed, 1975; Byres, 1986). Post-land reform agricultural growth aided the process of industrialisation in both these countries. Comparative studies between East Asia and Latin America have argued that the absence of land reform was one of the major reasons why Latin America was left behind in industrialisation (Kay, 2002).

To the contrary, agrarian relations in large parts of post-1947 India are marked by the absence of any radical transformation. In India, especially its Eastern regions, the British colonisers tried to 'introduce' the classical English path from the end of the 18th century. The Zamindari system was described by Marx as 'a caricature of English landlordism'. But far from promoting capitalism, the Zamindari system promoted a class of parasitic landlords. In other parts of India, the ryotwari system was introduced, which resembled 'French peasant-proprietorship'. Even ryotwari systems did not exclude landlordism, as the experience in south India, such as in Thanjavur and Malabar, show. The outcome was an absolute impover-ishment of the agricultural population and the stagnation of agricultural output in India (Habib, 2006).

In the post-1947 India, only a radical transformation of land relations through land reforms could ensure the elimination of landlordism, protection of tenant rights to land and finally, encourage the growth of capitalist relations in agriculture, which would ensure adequate supplies of wage goods and raw materials for industrialisation.

However, agricultural policy in India never really considered the reform of property rights in land as a means of eliminating structural inequalities in the economy and expanding the home market (Chakravarty, 1973; Patnaik, 1986; Rao, 1994). Land reforms in India have been a major failure. Ramachandran (2007) notes that 'working with a ceiling of 25 acres a household, no less than 63 million acres of land would have been available in the mid-1950s and early-1960s for distribution among landless and land-poor farmer households.' However, only 4.89 million acres of land have been distributed till 2006–07.

The absence of an agrarian revolution in India did not just slow down the growth of agricultural surplus; it also slowed down the mass expansion of literacy and school education, allowed the material basis of caste discrimination to persist and weakened the democratic content of local self-governments.

In the period of economic 'reforms' after 1991, land reform in India has been officially discarded. The basic premise of economic reform has been that with increased openness, the barriers to raising agricultural surplus could be overcome, not through land reform, but through external trade. The need for land reform did not just take a backseat; the effort was to reverse the implementation of land reform altogether.[8] Land ceiling laws in many States have been repealed to make way for large agribusiness-oriented cultivation units (Ramachandran and Ramakumar, 2000; Athreya, 2003). Such policies are likely to accelerate the loss of land by small peasants and further worsen inequalities in the distribution of land. In sum, the task of land reform, with all its complex local variations, remains central to the agrarian agenda of backward economies, such as India's.

PRE-CAPITALIST RELATIONSHIPS

Marx's discussion on pre-capitalist relationships appears in Chapter 36 in Volume III of *Capital*. In this chapter, Marx deals with a *form of capital* found in pre-capitalist societies — namely usurer's capital — and its role in the process of historical change. As a general term, Marx calls usurer's capital as *interest-bearing capital*; but usurer's capital, in pre-capitalist societies, is the 'antiquated form' of interest-bearing capital.[9]

Usurer's Capital

Prior to the capitalist mode of production, money was not closely attached to commodity production. When money is less attached to commodity production and the generation of exchange values, the more it appears only as wealth — a 'means of payment' that takes the 'absolute form of commodities'. Money starts to command an interest for its use and becomes 'money-capital'. In pre-capitalist societies, as the feudal mode of production begins to decay, there are two 'characteristic forms' that usurer's capital takes. First, extravagant members of the upper classes, such as the landlords, need money to continue with their squandering and decadent ways as well as to repay other debts that they have incurred. Secondly, small peasant proprietors — the majority — need money to make payments, as rents to landlords and taxes to the state get more and more monetized.

Here, usurer's capital sets in, and so does the usurer — the 'professional hoarder', who transforms his hoard of money into capital. When the small peasant or the small artisan confronts usurer's capital, they do so as producers. Whenever the costs of inputs rise abnormally or when there are crop failures, it becomes very difficult to repay debt. In a passage with much contemporary relevance in India, Marx writes:

> In individual cases the maintenance or loss of the means of production on the part of small producers depends on a thousand contingencies,

and every one of these contingencies or losses signifies impoverishment and becomes a crevice into which a parasitic usurer may creep. The mere death of his cow may render the small peasant incapable of renewing his reproduction on its former scale. He then falls into the clutches of the usurer, and once in the usurer's power he can never extricate himself. (*Capital,* III, p. 599)

Thus, usurer's capital becomes a means of appropriating surplus labour of producers and securing their conditions of labour, such as land and houses. It continuously expropriates the small producer. Similarly, usury economically drains the rich owners of large estates, and in many cases ruins them through debt. This process has ominous implications for the mode of production; it 'impoverishes the mode of production' and 'paralyses the productive forces'.

Yet, even while it centralises money wealth, usurer's capital does not directly subordinate labour to itself, or develop the social productivity of labour at the expense of labour itself; 'the mode of production still remains the same' (*Capital,* III, p. 596).[10] It is 'only where and when other prerequisites of capitalist production are present,' does usury contribute to the total ruin of the feudal mode of production and herald the capitalist mode of production.[11]

The Reaction Against Usury
Once the capitalist mode of production sets in, usury generates a reaction from the modern credit system. Now, interest-bearing capital qualitatively changes its form and becomes subordinated to the conditions and requirements of the capitalist mode of production. Usury can persist under capitalism only under two situations: first, in the 'backward branches of industry' or those branches that 'resist the transition to the modern mode of production' (*Capital,* III, p. 597); secondly, among those classes whose functions do not strictly correspond to the capitalist mode of production:

> ... where borrowing takes place as a result of individual need, as at the pawnshop; where money is borrowed by wealthy spendthrifts for the purpose of squandering; or where the producer is a non-capitalist producer, such as a small farmer or craftsman, who is thus still, as the immediate producer, the owner of his own means of production; finally where the capitalist producer himself operates on such a small

scale that he resembles those self-employed producers. (*Capital*, III, p. 600)

Under conditions of developing capitalism, the modern credit system — banks — develops as a counter to usury. Marx quotes a source noting that the Bank of England 'was a necessity for the government itself, sucked dry by usurers, in order to obtain money at a reasonable rate' (*Capital*, III, p. 602, ff). Against the Bank of England, 'all goldsmiths and pawnbrokers set up a howl of rage' (*Capital*, III, p. 603). Under industrial capitalism, the new banker played a dual social role. On the one hand, he mobilized the fragmented sources of capital and centralized that capital. On the other hand, he made available this centralized capital to the industrial capitalist, who was looking for large sums of credit. In this centralizing role under capitalism, banks did not allow any money to remain unproductive; they immediately 'capitalized' the money for the capitalist. However, such a transformation also contains within it the seeds of crisis (see Jayati Ghosh's essay in this volume).

Illustration from India

Usury was a major feature of agrarian relations in colonial India. Two factors created conditions for usurer's capital to flourish. First, the colonial state had begun to insist on the payment of rent by peasants in cash, and not in kind, due to which the produce had to be sold to traders in the market (Habib, 2006).[12] Secondly, in many regions, the timing of rent payment was fixed to be just before the harvest, or so close to the harvest that the peasant was forced to borrow (Patnaik, 2007). In the absence of a formal banking system, peasants and labourers were forced to depend on moneylenders and traders for advances.

The systematic development of a formal credit system in India began only in 1969, when 14 commercial banks were nationalised. Nationalisation of banks was primarily an attempt to develop a modern banking system based on the rule of law, which would displace the moneylender from Indian villages. Indeed, the policy helped to mop up the new liquidity in rural India after the green revolution, improve the geographical spread and functional reach of public banks and weaken the hold of usurious moneylenders (Shetty, 1997; Ramachandran and Swaminathan, 2005; Chavan, 2002). Such a banking policy aided the growth of capitalism in Indian agriculture.

Financial liberalisation in India after 1991 has undone much of the gains of bank nationalisation. After 1991, there was a decline of banking penetration and a return of the moneylender in rural India (Ramachandran and Swaminathan, 2005; Chavan, 2007; Ramakumar and Chavan, 2010, forthcoming). Official policy has moved away from directing credit to the small and marginal farmers; instead, it now openly encourages channeling farm credit to corporate and partnership houses for agri-business activities (Ramakumar and Chavan, 2007). The objective of displacing the moneylender has been dropped; instead, legislation for the registration of moneylenders is being planned. Banks are being asked to make use of the 'dominant presence' of moneylenders by providing them with incentives.

RENT IN AGRICULTURE

The discussion on rent in *Capital* appears in Volume III as well as in Part II of *Theories of Surplus Value* (TSV). Marx's treatment of capitalist rent in agriculture corrected an erroneous treatment of rent in the work of David Ricardo (see Patnaik, 2007). Patnaik's essay is a detailed analysis of the discussion of rent in Ricardo and Marx. In this sub-section, I shall confine myself to introducing Marx's concepts of (a) differential rent and (b) absolute rent. Marx discusses these two forms of ground rent after discussing labour rent and rent-in-kind, which are features of pre-capitalist societies. In other words, for Marx, ground rent is primarily a feature of the capitalist society.

Differential Rent
Agriculture is characterised by the *limitedness of land*. However, as Lenin pointed out, limitedness of land does not imply limitedness of land productivity; 'limitedness of the productivity of the land implies 'limitedness' of the given technical level, the given state of the productive forces' (Lenin, 1964a). As capitalism develops and the share of population employed in industry increases, the increased demand for food extends cultivation into new lands with varying levels of fertility. The average market value of food, in such conditions, gets derived from the value of food at the *worst fertile land*. The reason, as Marx notes, is that the presence of landed property in agriculture changes the way the social formation of value takes place in agriculture (see Fine, 1979 and Ghosh, 1985 for a discussion).

As different plots of land differ in levels of fertility, there would be more fertile plots that provide a higher-than-average profit to the tenant, as cultivation is undertaken at lower than the market-value. As the tenant has to pay rent, the surplus profit gets added to the rent paid to the landlord. This rent was termed by Marx as *differential rent.* In other words, differential rent is the excess of the rate of profit, over its average, that accrues to the landlord owing to the differences in the fertility (in industry, such differences are transient, as competition among capitalists would generalise the better method of production). Thus, differential rent (DR) would continue to exist even if the capitalist system is transcended.

Marx categorised DR into two types: DRI and DRII. The difference between DRI and DRII is a matter of the assumptions made in estimation. Under DRI, the variations in rent are explained by the application of equal quantities of capital to lands of differing fertilities. Here, purely natural fertility differences are the source of surplus profits. Under DRII, the variations in rent are explained by the application of unequal quantities of capital to lands of the same fertility. Capitals are unequal not because they are of their different *sizes.* Capitals are unequal because they have different *capabilities* to raise productivity and surplus profits (such as the ability to obtain credit). Here, the inequality across capitals in their ability to raise yields is the source of surplus profits. In Volume III of *Capital,* Marx undertakes a detailed exposition of the differences between DRI and DRII, and then tries to quantitatively determine DR in situations where DRI and DRII interact, as they do in actually given situations of unequal capital *and* unequal fertility.

In Ricardo's analysis, rent is simply determined according to the last unit of capital applied. In Marx's analysis, Ricardo's scenario is only a special case in the estimation of DRII.

If DR can be taken away from the landowner and given to the tenant, through limited tenancy reforms or larger land reforms, the tenant can use that part of the surplus profit too for investment in land. It is to be remembered that DR does not disappear after tenancy reform; it is just that it accrues to the tenant instead of the landowner.

Absolute Rent

In Ricardo's formulation, DR was the only form of rent in agriculture and there could be no land that yields food in its natural state and would not pay a DR. Marx, on the other hand, argued that the existence of 'landed property as a limitation continues to exist even when rent in the form of differential rent disappears (*Capital,* III, p. 751).

To illustrate the persistence of rent, Marx points to the 'worst' land, where only the average profit is produced and there is no scope for a surplus profit above the average profit. Will the landowner allow the tenant to keep the average profit and take no rent for himself? The nature of landed property in agriculture would undermine such a possibility. As a result, the selling price of food rises above the price of production to cover for the rent to be paid, and would range between the price of production (at the minimum) and its value (at the maximum). The difference between the price of production and the selling price is called *absolute rent* (AR).

The idea of formation of values and prices through the competition between capitals is central to the Marxian discussion on rent (Fine, 1979). As discussed by Marx in Part II of *TSV*, the transformation of values into prices is a two-stage process. In the first stage, the competition between capitals *within a sphere of production* determines market values of commodities. As a result, unequal rates of profit would prevail across sectors. In the second stage, the competition between capitals *across different spheres of production*, in search of the higher profits, leads to the formation of prices along with equalised rates of profits across sectors.

Agriculture, as a sphere of production or sector, is marked by low organic composition of capital, when compared to other sectors. A low organic composition of capital implies that values — determined by the average labour time required to produce it — and profit margins are higher in agriculture. Given higher profit margins, capital would tend to flow into agriculture and should ideally lead to the equalisation of rates of profit across sectors. However, Marx argued that the presence of landed property and its monopoly in agriculture, regardless of its *forms*, acts as a barrier to the equalisation of rates of profit across sectors. This phenomenon is unique to agriculture, as landed property does not exist in industry.

As monopolistic landed property becomes a barrier to the equalisation of profits, agricultural products would sell at a price higher than the price of production.[13] Equalisation of profits, and thus a reduction of price, can be achieved only if landed property is abolished. Only then can we also ensure that all the barriers to new investment in agriculture are eliminated. As Marx explained to Engels in a letter in 1862,

> ... it is by no means *essential* for *absolute rent* to be paid under all circumstances or in respect of *every type of soil* ... It is not paid when *landed property* does *not* exist, either factually or legally. In such a case, agriculture offers no peculiar resistance to the application of capital,

which then moves as easily in this element as in the other. The agricultural produce is then sold, as masses of industrial products always are, *at cost price* for *less* than its value. In practice, *landed property* may disappear, even when capitalist and landowner is one and the same person . . . . (Marx, 1862/1913, available at http://www.marxists.org/archive/marx/works/1862/letters/62_08_02.htm)

The solution in actual policy is the nationalisation of land, which would abolish ground rent, and allow the free penetration of capital into agriculture (see Lenin, 1977; Kautsky, 1988). As Lenin wrote on the implications of land nationalisation vis-à-vis ground rent:

> . . . the question of the nationalisation of the land in capitalist society is divided into two materially different parts: the question of differential rent, and the question of absolute rent. Nationalisation changes the owner of the former, and undermines the very existence of the latter. Hence, on the one hand, nationalisation is a partial reform within the limits of capitalism (a change of owners of a part of surplus value), and on the other hand, it abolishes the monopoly which hinders the whole development of capitalism in general. (Lenin, 1977, p. 79)

Even if land is not nationalised, it would be possible to reduce AR substantially with thoroughgoing land reform, where a large number of small producers would own plots of land adequate for their reproduction.

Ground Rent and the Agrarian Question in India

E.M.S. Namboodiripad (EMS) was one of the few Indian scholars to have analysed India's agrarian question in the context of Marx's analysis of ground rent (see Namboodiripad, 1940 and 1984). Namboodiripad (1984) is a larger analysis of Indian agrarian situation, and Namboodiripad (1940) is EMS's famous minute of dissent as a member of the Kuttikrishna Menon Committee in 1939, which examined the agrarian situation in Malabar. Both these articles are a must-read for any student of India's agrarian question. As Patnaik (1999) points out, EMS's 1984 article was a response to two extreme arguments; one, the Naxalite argument that characterised Indian agriculture as 'semi-feudal'; two, the revisionist view within the Left that saw the bourgeois revolution in land as already carried out through land reforms, thus denying all pre-capitalist remnants.

In a detailed reading of *Capital* and *TSV*, EMS pointed out to the revisionists that it was their lack of grasp of ground rent that led them to conclude that the bourgeois revolution in land was complete. To the extremists, he pointed out the continuing growth of capitalism in Indian agriculture, even while it preserved a number of pre-capitalist elements in the form of Junker-style landlord-capitalists.

According to EMS, India's agrarian transition is far from complete, given that neither is the labourer paid a wage equal to the value of his labour power nor is the tenant farmer earning an average profit for his investment. Hence, the ground rent in India is not a fully capitalist ground rent. The landlord's rent also includes a part of the normal wage of the worker and a part of the profit of the small tenant farmer. While this indicates 'the heritage of the pre-capitalist order', commodity production in agriculture has also, alongside, expanded significantly. EMS uses Marx's example of Ireland in *Capital*, which had a different trajectory of capitalist development compared to England; in India, as in Ireland of Marx's times, 'landed property in the capitalist mode of production formally exists without the existence of the capitalist mode of production itself'. He wrote:

> Landlord's rent in India is thus capitalist Ground Rent in form but continues to retain in its essence the characteristics of all its pre-capitalist predecessors. (Namboodiripad, 1984, p. 11)[14]

EMS further noted, drawing from Kautsky's (1988) analysis of ground rent, that 'the rent appropriated by the landlord has assumed its new capitalised form, i.e., the price of land' (p. 11). The high price of land also militates against land being exchanged freely in the market, and consequently, allowing new investment to take place in land.

As EMS noted, Marx's arguments related to capitalist ground rent can not be applied schematically to the Indian case, where the capitalist transition is incomplete. Ghosh (1985) has argued that the concept of AR can be studied as an important element in cases where capitalist cultivation co-exists with peasant farming for subsistence. Here, she treats AR as 'essentially pre-capitalist rent', which is determined by the relative bargaining power of landlords and tenants. Ghosh considers the case of United Provinces in India during the colonial period, and notes that there were major barriers to the entry of capitalist farmers given the stiff structuring of rents that inhibited fresh investments in land. However, these barriers were weakened between the 1860s and 1930s in the western regions of United Provinces through a number of factors:

> . . . the increased profitability of cultivation resulting from commercialisation; the growth of the export market and the secular rise in product prices from 1870 to 1930; the operation of state legislation which created a category of legally privileged (occupancy) tenants who could pay substantially lower rent rates than those competitively prevailing; and the growing importance of DR-I resulting from irrigation and transport networks, not all of which was incorporated into the competitive rent rates. (Ghosh 1985, p. 80)

None of these forces were powerful enough in the eastern regions of United Provinces to help overcome the barriers to investment set by pre-capitalist rents. Consequently, the eastern regions remained agriculturally backward through the colonial period. Thus, Ghosh argues that Marx's absolute rent could also be conceptualised to analyse agrarian economies that are in the process of transition to the capitalist organisation of agriculture.[15]

CONCLUDING NOTES

Our discussion of the treatment of agriculture in Marx's *Capital* underlines the continuing need to view the resolution of India's agrarian question as the foremost national question before the Indian people. Addressing the agrarian question requires land reform, which would abolish landlordism as well as end exploitation by merchants and moneylenders in the countryside. Land reform would also remove the barriers to investment in agriculture and expand the home market. In India's specific conditions, land reform also has the historic task of weakening the material basis of upper caste-hegemony in the villages.

Marx's *Capital* is, thus, an important guide in the struggles of peasant movements, agricultural labour movements and movements of oppressed castes.

REFERENCES

Ahmed, Zahir (1975), *Land Reforms in South-East Asia*, Orient Longman, New Delhi.

Athreya, Venkatesh, Djurfeldt, Goran and Lindberg, S. (1990), *Barriers Broken: Production Relations and Agrarian Change in Tamil Nadu*, Sage Publications, New Delhi.

Athreya, Venkatesh (2003), 'Redistributive Land Reforms in India: Some Reflections in the Current Context', Paper Presented in the All-India Conference on *Agriculture and Rural Society in Contemporary India*, Barddhaman, December 17–20.

Bhaduri, Amit (1983), *The Economic Structure of Bbackward Agriculture*, Academic Press, London.

Breman, Jan (1974), *Patronage and Exploitation: Changing Agrarian Relations in South Gujarat*, University of California Press, Berkeley.

Brenner, Robert (1976), 'Agrarian Class Structure and Economic Development in Pre-Industrial Europe', *Past and Present*, 70, February.

Brenner, Robert (2004), 'What Is, and What Is Not, Imperialism?', *Historical Materialism*, 14 (4), pp. 79–105.

Byres, Terence J. (1986) 'The Agrarian Question, Forms of Capitalist Agrarian Transition and the State: An Essay with Reference to Asia', *Social Scientist*, 14 (11–12), pp. 3–67.

Chakravarty, Sukhamoy (1973), *Writings on Development*, Oxford University Press, New Delhi.

Chavan, Pallavi (2002), *Some Features of Rural Credit in India with Special Reference to Tamil Nadu: A Study of the Period after Bank Nationalisation*, M. Phil. Thesis, Indira Gandhi Institute of Development Research, Mumbai.

Chavan, Pallavi (2007), 'Access to Bank Credit: Implications for Dalit Rural Households', *Economic and Political Weekly*, August 4.

Dobb, Maurice (1963), *Studies in the Development of Capitalism*, Routledge and Kegan Paul, London and Henley.

Dore, Ronald (1959), *Land Reform in Japan*, Oxford University Press, London.

Fine, Ben (1979), 'On Marx's Theory of Agricultural Rent', *Economy and Society*, 8 (3), pp. 241–278.

Fine, Ben (2004), 'Debating the 'New' Imperialism', *Historical Materialism*, 14 (4), pp. 133–156.

Ghosh, Jayati (1985), 'Differential and Absolute Land Rent', *Journal of Peasant Studies*, 13 (11), pp. 67–82.

Habib, Irfan (1969), 'Potentialities of Capitalistic Development in the Economy of Mughal India', *The Journal of Economic History*, 29 (1), pp. 32–78.

Habib, Irfan (1995), 'Capitalism in History', *Social Scientist*, 23 (7/9), pp. 15–31.

Habib, Irfan (2006), 'Colonialism and the Indian Economy', in *Indian Economy, 1858–1914*, Tulika Books, New Delhi, pp. 23–50.

Harriss, John (1982), *Capitalism and Peasant Farming; Agrarian Change and Ideology in Northern Tamil Nadu*, Oxford University Press, New Delhi.

Harvey, David (2003), *The New Imperialism*, Oxford University Press, Oxford.

Harvey, David (2007), 'Reflections: David Harvey interviewed by Alberto Toscano,' *Development and Change*, 38 (6), pp. 1127–1135.

Hobsbawm, Eric (1962), *The Age of Revolution: Europe, 1789–1848*, Abacus, London.

Hobsbawm, Eric (1968), *Industry and Empire: From 1750 to the Present Day*, Pelican Books, London.

Hobsbawm, Eric and Rude, George (1973), *Captain Swing*, Phoenix Press, London.

Kautsky, Karl (1988), *The Agrarian Question*, Swan Books, Winchester.

Kay, Cristobal (2002), 'Why East Asia overtook Latin America: Agrarian Reform, Industrialisation and Development', *Third World Quarterly*, 23 (6), pp 1073–1102.

Kothari, Smitu and Harcourt, Wendy (2004), 'Introduction: The Violence of Development', *Development*, 47 (1), pp. 3–7.

Lenin, V. I. (1964a), 'New Data on the Laws Governing the Development of Capitalism in Agriculture', Lenin's *Collected Works*, Progress Publishers, Moscow, Volume 22, pp. 13–102.

Lenin, V. I. (1964b), *The Development of Capitalism in Russia*, Progress Publishers, Moscow.

Lenin, V. I. (1977), *The Agrarian Programme of Social-Democracy in the First Russian Revolution, 1905–1907*, Progress Publishers, Moscow.

Mies, Maria and Shiva, Vandana (1993), *Ecofeminism*, Zed Books, London.

Mundle, Sudipto (1979), *Backwardness and Bondage: Agrarian Relations in a South Bihar district*, Indian Institute of Public Administration, New Delhi.

Nagaraj, K. (1981), *Structure and Inter-Relations of the Land, Labour, Credit and Product Markets of South Kanara*, Ph. D. thesis, Indian Statistical Institute, Kolkata.

Namboodiripad, E. M. S. (1940), Dissenting Note in *Report of the Malabar Tenancy Committee – 1940*, Government of Madras, Madras, in *Selected Writings*, Volume 2, National Book Agency, Calcuttta. Reprinted in E.M.S. Namboodiripad, *History, Society and Land Relations: Selected Essays*, LeftWord, New Delhi, 2010.

Namboodiripad, E. M. S. (1983), 'The Marxist Theory of Ground Rent: Relevance to the Study of Agrarian Question in India', *Social Scientist*, 12 (2), pp. 3–15. Reprinted in E.M.S. Namboodiripad, *History, Society and Land Relations: Selected Essays*, LeftWord, New Delhi, 2010.

Patnaik, Utsa (1983), 'Classical Theory of Rent and its Application to India: Some Preliminary Propositions, with Some Thoughts on Sharecropping', *Journal of Peasant Studies*, 10 (2–3).

Patnaik, Utsa (1985), 'The Agrarian Question and Development of Capitalism in India', *Economic and Political Weekly*, 21 (18), pp. 781–793.

Patnaik, Utsa (1999), 'EMS on the Agrarian Question: Ground Rent and Its Implications', *Social Scientist*, 27 (9/10), pp. 51–64.

Patnaik, Utsa (2006), 'The Free Lunch: Transfers from the Tropical Colonies and their Role in Capital Formation in Britain during the Industrial Revolution', in Jomo K. S. (ed.), *Globalization under Hegemony: The Changing World Economy*, Tulika Books, New Delhi.

Patnaik, Utsa (2007), 'Introduction', in *The Agrarian Question in Marx and His Successors*, Volume 1, Leftword Books, New Delhi.

Patnaik, Utsa and Dingwaney, Manjari (eds.) (1985), *Chains of Servitude: Bondage and Slavery in India*, Sangam Books, Madras.

Ramachandran, V. K (1990), *Wage Labour and Unfreedom in Agriculture: An Indian Case Study*, Clarendon Press, Oxford, New York.

Ramachandran, V. K. (2007), 'Agrarian Relations: The Lynchpin', *The Hindu*, August 15.

Ramachandran, V. K. and Ramakumar, R. (2000), 'Agrarian Reforms and Rural Development Policies in India: A Note', Paper presented at the International Conference on *Agrarian Reform and Rural Development*, Department of Agrarian Reform, Government of the Philippines and the Philippines Development Academy, Tagaytay City, December 5 to 8 (published in a conference volume).

Ramachandran, V. K. and Swaminathan, Madhura (2002), 'Rural Banking and Landless Labour Households: Institutional Reform and Rural Credit Markets in India', *Journal of Agrarian Change*, 2 (4), October.

Ramachandran, V. K. and Swaminathan, Madhura (eds.) (2005), *Financial Liberalisation and Rural Credit in India*, Tulika Books, New Delhi.

Ramakumar, R and Chavan, Pallavi (2007), 'Revival of Agricultural Credit in the 2000s: An Explanation', *Economic and Political Weekly*, 42 (52), December 29, 2007, pp. 57–64.

Ramakumar, R and Chavan, Pallavi (2010, forthcoming), 'Changes in the Number of Rural Bank Branches in India, 1991 to 2008', *Review of Agrarian Studies*, 1 (1).

Ramakumar, R. (2004), 'Socioeconomic Characteristics of Agricultural Workers: A Case Study in the Malabar Region of Kerala', Ph. D. Thesis, Indian Statistical Institute, Kolkata.

Rao, J. Mohan (1994), 'Agricultural Development under State Planning', in Terence J. Byres (ed.), *The State, Development Planning and Liberalisation in India*, Oxford University Press, New Delhi.

Rao, J. Mohan (1999), 'Freedom, Equality, Property and Bentham: The Debate over Unfree Labour', *Journal of Peasant Studies*, 27 (1), pp. 97–127.

Rawal, Vikas (2006), 'The Labour Process in Rural Haryana (India): A Field-Report from Two Villages', *Journal of Agrarian Change*, 6 (4), October, pp. 538–583.

Rawal, Vikas and Osmani, Siddiqur (2010), 'Economic Policies, Tenancy Relations and Household Incomes: Insights from Three Selected Villages in India', Unpublished paper, University of Ulster, Ulster.

Shetty, S. L (1997), 'Financial Sector Reforms in India: An Evaluation', *Prajnan*, 25 (3–4), pp. 253–287.

Singh, Manmohan (2004), 'India: The Next Decade', Speech at The Indira Gandhi Conference, New Delhi, November 19, available at http://pmindia.nic.in/speech/content4print.asp?id=47.

Soboul, Albert (1956), 'The French Rural Community in the Eighteenth and Nineteenth Centuries', *Past and Present*, 10, November, pp. 78–95.

Thorner, Daniel and Alice Thorner (1962) *Land and Labour in India*, Asia Publishers, Mumbai.

NOTES

1 I would like to thank a number of colleagues and friends who helped in writing this essay. Venkatesh Athreya and J. Mohan Rao read a first draft and gave detailed suggestions on the arguments and presentation. Vikas Rawal, Sudhanva Deshpande and Vineet Kohli also read the draft of the essay and gave comments. Discussions with T. Jayaraman helped me sharpen some of the main arguments. The usual disclaimer applies. All references to *Capital* are from the LeftWord Books edition, New Delhi, 2010.

2 It is important to note here that in many pre-capitalist societies, 'free' petty proprietors and 'free' wage labourers were an important presence. Conditions of freedom in pre-capitalist societies are historically specified, and not always amenable to generalisation.

3 In his writings on capitalism, David Harvey (2003) has introduced a concept called 'accumulation by dispossession' (AbD), where he expands the concept

of primitive accumulation. For Harvey, AbD is the process of taking away people's rights to dispose of their own resources, and it is a process that could be repeated even under advanced global capitalism (thus, not just being its starting point). The evidence, for Harvey, is the predatory movements of metropolitan capital into backward societies in the process of imperialist advance. AbD, for Harvey, includes a wide range of contentious contemporary issues, from intellectual property rights to privatization, growth of MNCs, the Iraq war, and environmental degradation.

Harvey's conceptual framework has been subjected to rigorous critical scrutiny. First, Harvey's argument can sustain itself only on the doubtful assumption that all the possibilities of internal expansion of capitalism are exhausted, leaving the capture of non-capitalist external markets as the only feasible route for global capitalism to expand. As Ben Fine (2006, p. 143) puts it, there is thus a 'confusion over the relationship between the internal and external' in Harvey's work. Secondly, the concept of primitive accumulation was advanced by Marx for a specific historical stage during the origins of capitalism. Indeed, forcible processes of expropriation of either individual or communal rights do continue long after the genesis of capitalism and even of its spread on a global scale. However, rather than analyzing the new forms of expropriation as normal processes of capitalist expansion, Harvey extends the concept of primitive accumulation to the advanced stages and includes under its ambit a number of disparate, diverse and complex trends in capital accumulation that we notice around us. Critics have argued that such characterization amounts to a 'conflation of the analytical categories' (Fine, 2006, p. 145). As Robert Brenner (2006, p. 102) asks in a critical note: 'Why inflate the concept out of existence?'

4 There are a number of important field-work based writings on freedom and unfreedom of agricultural labourers in India. A point that many of these studies have emphasised is that, given the absence of any decisive agrarian reforms, the transition from unfree to free labour relations in India can not be characterised as 'one or the other', and that it is a slow and gradual process (see Breman, 1974; Ramachandran, 1990). Breman's and Ramachandran's studies of villages in south Gujarat and Tamil Nadu, respectively, showed how, even in a situation where wage labour predominated, labour relations could be marked by the vestiges of traditional forms of servitude in various degrees. As Ramachandran argued, 'socio-economic life in the village is a complex web of inter-relationships; there is an immense variety of bonds that link the agricultural labourer to the landlord' (1990, p. 175), and 'individual agricultural labourers may move between different positions on a freedom-unfreedom scale' (1990, p. 251). See also Thorner and Thorner (1962); Mundle (1979); Nagaraj (1981); Harriss (1982); Bhaduri (1983); Patnaik and Dingwaney (1985); Athreya *et al* (1990); Rawal (2006); and Ramakumar (2006).

5 This is not to imply that the bourgeoisie will not use the state apparatus under

advanced capitalism to drive down wages or intensify labour. It does, and it uses the global imperialist system to this end as well.

6 British colonialism also wrecked havoc in the lives of majority of people in India. Marx particularly notes that in 1866, 'more than a million Hindus died of hunger in the province of Orissa alone' (V-I, *ff*. p. 753).

7 For a treatment of the French path of transition, where small peasant proprietors were not swept away as in England, see Soboul (1956) and Byres (1986).

8 In a recent address, Prime Minister Manmohan Singh noted that while agrarian India must be transformed into a viable and modern economy, 'it has to be appreciated that the scope for a successful classical land reform involving large-scale redistribution of land is very limited' (Singh, 2004).

9 Indeed, in many medieval societies, usury was legally banned for many religious and cultural reasons. Yet, the compliance to these laws varied in degree.

10 In many cases, usurers were representatives of the pre-capitalist order itself: large landowners or merchants.

11 For a theorisation of usury in under-developed rural credit markets, see Bhaduri (1983).

12 The first impetus to the monetization of peasant rents in India, however, predates British colonial rule to the period of Mughal rule. Habib (1969) writes that 'in Mughal India, our evidence indicates quite plainly that collection of revenue in cash was far more prevalent than collection in kind' (p. 39).

13 It has been argued that Marx's framework in which agricultural commodities are sold at their values is incomplete, as it does not satisfactorily clarify as to why the value should act as an upper ceiling in the determination of sale price (see Ghosh, 1985). However, Marx did concede that the forces of demand and supply may play a role in agricultural commodities ultimately selling at *below* their values: 'whether the rent equals the entire difference between the value and the price of production, or only a greater a lesser part of it, will depend wholly on the relation between supply and demand and on the area of land newly taken under cultivation' (V-III, pp. 762-763).

14 For an application of the classical theory of rent to sharecropping in India, see Patnaik (1983).

15 See Rawal and Osmani (2010) for a recent analysis of tenancy relations using data from three villages in India. They note the persistence of 'exploitative tenancy contracts' in the villages, which were 'sustained on the basis of a high degree of landlessness, low levels of availability of wage employment, and lack of access of asset poor households to formal-sector credit.' (p. 26).

The Three Stories of *Capital* and their Relevance Today

Prasenjit Bose

Karl Marx developed his critique of capitalism, by critiquing the ideas dominating political economy of his times through a large body of economic manuscripts written in the 1850s. His critique eventually culminated in *Capital*, published in 1867, where his philosophical framework, conceptual tools and political economy analysis of capitalism, were brought together in their entirety.[1] It was Marx's masterpiece, the zenith of his creative genius.

But why should we be interested in *Capital* today, a century and a half after it was written? The French Marxist philosopher Louis Althusser wrote in the early 1970s that just as the Greeks in the fifth century B.C. 'opened up' to scientific knowledge the 'Continent of Mathematics' and Galileo 'the Continent of Physics', Marx's critique of political economy opened up to scientific knowledge the 'Continent of History'.[2]

But if it is a book on the history of capitalism, how is it of interest to those who do not study history? It is interesting because it tells the history of capitalism as a social system, in a totally novel and unconventional manner. It does not narrate the history of specific nations, or their rulers and subjects; or specific events of great import like wars, conquests or the rise and fall of civilizations. What it does is to first meticulously build up concepts like surplus value, class exploitation, commodity production, reproduction and accumulation of capital; and then rewrite the history of modern society through these concepts.

Marx, moreover, believed that the 'point' of philosophy is not merely to '*interpret*' the world but to '*change*' it.[3] This radical objective always remained at the core of all the work that he produced, *Capital* being its most rigorous and pristine manifestation. Such was the profundity of Marx's analysis and the power of his critique, that it unleashed a revolutionary movement against capitalism across the globe, in search for alternatives to the capitalist order. The ebbs and flows of that movement shaped much of world history of the twentieth century.

Skeptics, however, ask today: hasn't capitalism proved to be far more enduring than what Marx had predicted? Hasn't capitalism changed dramatically over the past century rendering Marxist concepts outdated? What purpose does *Capital's* analysis serve in the globalized world of the twenty first century? This essay addresses these critical questions. But before we embark on them, let us see what Marx had to say about capitalism in *Capital.*

THREE STORIES OF *CAPITAL*

The initial chapters of the first volume of *Capital* deal with abstract conceptual categories, which form the building blocks for the critical and rich analysis of capitalism contained in the later chapters. The second and third volumes expand upon specific themes, which have been developed in the first volume. All this makes *Capital* a difficult text.[4] One can, however, read into its complex narrative, three fairly simple but fascinating stories, which we narrate below. These distinct but interconnected stories are constructed primarily from the first volume of *Capital,* with parts of the second story drawing from the second and third volumes. These are of course not the *only* stories contained in *Capital,* and the present volume itself is testimony to the myriad stories contained in this master work. We have chosen these only because of their acute contemporary relevance.

First Story: Class Exploitation

The starting point of the first story is that the realities of the world are not visible at its surface. More specifically, what is visible as the capitalist world around us is a veneer underneath which lies the actual apparatus that drives the system. The world at first sight appears to us as a gigantic marketplace, where commodities of various kinds are bought and sold by sellers and buyers. Commodities — which are necessary or useful to us in many ways — are bought and sold (exchanged) in markets at prices, which reflect their values. And money is the universal commodity, because it is accepted by everybody as the universal measure of value and therefore can be exchanged for all other commodities. So we tend to believe that value resides in the prices of commodities or in money. But from where does value originate? To understand this we have to delve deeper into the world of commodities to understand how these commodities come into being in the first place.

Once we delve into the sphere of production of commodities, we encounter a world very different from the sphere of exchange. Here commodities are produced from other commodities, either raw materials sourced from nature or finished products, which in turn have been produced from raw materials sourced from nature and so on. Thus each commodity embodies within itself several other commodities, the ultimate source of which being raw materials found in nature. What transforms raw materials into finished products, or one set of commodities into another set of commodities? It is the application of human labour. One can argue that the transformation of one set of commodities into another set of commodities cannot be achieved by applying labour alone. Labour has to be applied on a certain technique of production. But techniques are embodied in the means of production, like tools and machines. These means of production are also commodities, which have first been conceived or designed and then transformed from other commodities, with the application of labour.

Thus labour is central to the process of commodity production, since it alone has the capacity of transforming one commodity into another. In the process of producing commodities from raw materials, it is labour, which imparts value to it.[5] Despite this, labour is not valued in terms of its contribution under capitalism. Rather, it is also treated like a commodity. The workers sell labour — their labour power — against a wage. Moreover, this wage is determined not in terms of the value of the commodity produced by labour but merely in terms of what is enough to reproduce labour. In other words workers are paid a wage, which ensures their subsistence, but does not compensate fully for their contribution in the production process.

Why does this happen? Primarily because of the property relations under capitalism, wherein workers own nothing apart from their labour power and all means of production, i.e., all commodities other than labour power required for production, are owned by a handful of people, the capitalists. Thus, workers have no other choice but to sell their labour power to the capitalists for a wage in order to ensure their subsistence. The capitalists, by virtue of their ownership of all means of production, buy the workers' labour power for a wage, employ that labour to produce commodities and appropriate the commodities — the products of labour — in their entirety. What the workers get as wages is therefore only a fraction of the total value of their produce; the rest — surplus value — goes to the capitalists. This surplus value is realised as profit, when commodities are sold by the capitalists in the market at a per unit price, much higher than what has been paid as per unit wage to the workers. Thus, capital is not merely the sum total of the commodities and means of production owned by the capitalists. It embodies a social relationship, wherein capital itself is the product of surplus value extracted from labour. This in essence is the nature of class exploitation under capitalism.

Exploitation under capitalism does not arise out of the subjective attributes of individual owners of capital, i.e., not because capitalists are cruel or nasty. Exploitation of wage labour to extract surplus value and earn profit is the *raison d'etre* of capitalists. Moreover, the capitalists always want to expand their capital by maximizing their profits. The more the workers produce at a given wage, the more will be the rate at which surplus value is appropriated and therefore, higher the profits. One way of increasing profits by the capitalists is to lengthen the working day at a given wage. The other is to change the techniques of production in such manner as to increase the output produced by each worker in a given time period, i.e. increase the productivity of labour. Techniques of production undergo changes through the introduction of newer and more sophisticated machines, which automate production processes, rendering specific skills of workers redundant. The progressive decline in the skill requirements of labour draws in unskilled workers, women and children into the workforce and greatly facilitates the cheapening of labour.

Workers, on the other hand, resist attempts by the capitalists to increase the rate of surplus value and they try their utmost to increase their wages. This struggle between the workers and the capitalists for a greater share of the produce lies at the heart of the production process under capitalism. The system, however, is heavily loaded in favour of the capitalists. The strength of the workers in class struggle is limited by the fact that all other means of production are owned by the capitalists. Increasing automation of production further enhances capitalists' control over the production process. Moreover, the existence of a huge pool of unemployed persons under capitalism — the reserve army of labour — enables the capitalists to practise hire and fire, constraining the ability of the workers to press for higher wages. Thus, workers can increase their wages under capitalism once in a while, but overall they remain subjugated as 'wage slaves' of the capitalist class. The only way workers can get rid of wage slavery is by getting rid of the capitalist system itself.

Second Story: Accumulation and Crisis

This story, which runs parallel to the story of class exploitation, concerns the state of motion of capital. The world of commodities under capitalism experiences expansion over time, with commodities being produced and reproduced on an expanding scale. But capitalism also experiences frequent crises, when commodities find no buyers and the production process suddenly comes to a standstill. What accounts for these contradictory syndromes of dynamism and paralysis?

In the beginning of a production process, the capitalist employs labour along with the means of production to produce commodities, extracts surplus value by appropriating the produce and sells it to realize profit in the form of money. If the capitalist consumes the entire amount of money earned after the first round, there will be no capital left to employ labour for the second round. The process of production will come to a grinding halt after the initial round of production. Without production, there will be no profit for the capitalist to earn. Therefore, in order to sustain the production process as well as the flow of profits, the capitalist has to reinvest a part of the money earned after the first round in the production process for employing labour.

If the capitalist consumes only the amount earned as profit and reinvests the rest in the second period, exactly the same amount of commodities will be produced as in the first period, implying exactly the same amount of profit (simple reproduction). If the capitalist does not consume his entire profit earned at the end of the first period, and reinvests a part of it, capital employed in the second period will expand, employing more labour, producing more commodities and earning more profits at the end of the period (expanded reproduction). It is this expanded reproduction which occurs as a recursive process under capitalism: the capitalist employing his capital to produce commodities, earning profits by selling the commodities, re-employing a part of his profits as capital to produce more commodities, and so on. This is the process of capital accumulation, which gives capitalism its dynamic character.

Moreover, a capitalist, as noted in the first story itself, always wants to expand his capital by earning more profits. One way of increasing profits is to increase the rate of surplus value by lowering wages. But the subsistence level of workers set lower limits to wages, pushed beyond which the reproduction of labour itself will become impossible. The other way to earn more profits is to expand the scale of production. For this, the capitalist has to reinvest a greater part of his profit to employ more means of production and labour. This leads to an expansion in the production of commodities, more surplus value, more profits and at the end of the process, more money in the hands of the capitalist. This is the actual process of capital accumulation, whereby capital reproduces itself recursively on an extended scale. Through this process, money grows into more money, and wealth is accumulated by the capitalist class.

As far as the workers are concerned, expanded reproduction tends to absorb more labour. However, since the diminution of the reserve army of the unemployed would enhance the bargaining strength of the workers, who would start demanding more wages exerting downward pressure on profits, a progressive increase in the size of the workforce is not in the interest of the capitalists. Therefore, extended reproduction of capital is also accompanied by the introduction of labour saving techniques of production, whereby increase of output is achieved through increases in labour productivity. As a result, the wages of the workers continue to remain at their level of subsistence, while profits continue to rise. The overall social consequence of the accumulation process is therefore, the progressive enrichment of the capitalist class at the cost of the workers, who create all the wealth but earn only their subsistence.

The process of capital accumulation also concentrates wealth and means of production in the hands of individual capitalists, creating big blocs of capital. This on the one hand leads to increasing the scale of production and introduction of newer techniques, which increases the overall power of capital over labour. On the other hand it also leads to competition between individual capitalists, over selling more commodities and owning bigger blocs of capital. The competition between capitalists assumes a specific form whereby either a few big capitalists takeover the capital of many small capitalists or many small capitalists transform themselves into a few big ones. The end result is the creation of gigantic blocs of capital under capitalist enterprises, the process of centralization of capital.

In this process of big blocs of capital growing bigger by gobbling up smaller blocs of capital, a crucial role is played by the financial system under capitalism. Banks mobilize savings from individuals in society and lend it to capitalists, as capital, against a share in their profits (interest). The bigger blocs of capital utilize this additional capital made available by the financial system to outcompete and gobble up the smaller blocks. The process of centralization of capital also transforms capitalist production, through technological progress, into large-scale industrial establishments. A large number of workers come under one roof in these establishments and work with modern machinery to produce commodities on a massive scale.

While the process of capital accumulation imparts dynamism to capitalism and centralization transforms capitalism through technological innovations and industrial progress, these processes are ridden with contradictions. First, the benefits of industrial progress under capitalism largely accrue to capitalists as higher profits. This is ensured through the nature of technological progress itself, whereby labour productivity rises continuously, restraining employment growth. As a result, the reserve army of the unemployed persists preventing the workers from increasing their wages and securing a better share in the social produce.

Second, workers are also consumers under capitalism and, therefore, provide market for the capitalists to sell their commodities, without which profits cannot be realized. Limits on the share of the workers in the social produce set by the working of the capitalist system, also limits their income and purchasing power, thereby limiting the growth of the market. This makes the system prone to crises, characterized by over-production of commodities, which capitalists are unable to sell. When a crisis occurs, unsold commodities accumulate and profits dry up, making the capitalists unwilling to employ their capital. The entire accumulation process gets disrupted, resulting in closure of enterprises, workers losing jobs and unemployment growing rapidly. Capitalism comes out of such crisis only through a partial destruction of capital and much social suffering.

Third, while the poverty and restricted consumption of the working masses remain as the basic underlying cause of crisis under capitalism, the character of its financial system further complicates its predicament. Capital in order to grow requires credit, which by making money owned by others available to a capitalist, enables extended reproduction. In return, the creditors get a share of the capitalist's profit as interest, and grow in size over time. The 'superabundance' of this 'money-capital' (financial capital), however, enables it to acquire certain autonomous features, which in turn impact the capital accumulation process.

Money-capital expresses itself in a 'plethora' of financial assets other than cash, like stocks, bonds and mortgages, which are titles of ownership to tiny portions of real capital. These can be bought and sold with much more ease and frequency than an entire portion of real capital. Transactions of these titles as commodities, eventually lead to their values rising or falling independent of the value of the real capital on which these are titles of ownership, creating 'illusory' value. This provides avenues for speculation and gambling, which attracts more and more of money-capital into these transactions. This creates sharp inflation in asset prices, which artificially force an expansion in the reproduction process. When these artificially inflated prices eventually crash, there is a rush to sell financial assets and convert to cash. This causes credit to dry up because money capitalists become unwilling to lend, and as a result the reproduction process gets disrupted, precipitating crisis in both the spheres of financial and real capital.

The accumulation process under capitalism, therefore, contains contradictory tendencies of expansion and crisis. While extended reproduction of capital tends to expand the social produce, by revolutionizing the means of production, persisting unemployment and poverty of the workers — caused by the self-same production process — limits social consumption, and impedes continued reproduction. Again, centralization of capital concentrates enormous wealth and resources in the hands of capitalists. But superabundance of wealth leads to financial speculation and asset price inflation, which eventually precipitates crisis and destroys wealth and resources. Capitalism moves in time through these self-contradictory processes.

Third Story: The History of Capitalism
The production condition under capitalism is characterized by the exploitation of wage labour by the capital. But from where and how did this production condition originate? There cannot be any capitalist unless there is capital. But capital is produced through the exploitation of workers by capitalists. So who came first; capital, the capitalists or the workers? Actually, they all came together through the process of primitive accumulation of capital.

This process is 'primitive' in the sense that it precedes the emergence of capitalism. The feudal society comprised of an agricultural population, largely small peasants tilling land and sharing the produce with the feudal landlords. The process of primitive accumulation of capital entailed forced eviction of the peasants from their land and the usurpation of that land by a new class of landlords. This expropriation of the peasantry converted them into a propertyless mass of paupers — 'beggars, robbers, vagabonds' — from which the class of wage workers, i.e., the proletariat was born. The same process also converted land from feudal or common property into capitalist private property and unleashed capitalist development in agriculture by creating capitalist landlords and farmers. The advent of capitalism in agriculture not only destroyed small peasant production, but all other forms of small producers — 'weavers, spinners and artisans'– whose production was intricately linked with the agrarian economy. The destruction of petty production opened up the domestic market for industrial production.

The first industrial capitalists primarily originated from the class of merchants and moneylenders of Western Europe, besides some craftsmen who grew into capitalists over time. The accumulation of capital through trade and commerce eventually assumed the character of colonial conquests, loot and plunder of societies in America, Africa and Asia, involving massacres and enslavement of indigenous populations and expropriation of their natural resources and minerals through brute force. Ruthless colonial exploitation and slave trade was the main form of primitive accumulation of capital. The accumulation of 'national debt' by the government, and their repayment to the moneylenders and banks by extracting taxes from the masses, served as another means of primitive accumulation. It was through this violent process of primitive accumulation of capital — expropriation of peasants and other small producers, colonial exploitation, slave trade and slavery, taxation of the masses — that the capital for capitalism emerged, 'dripping from head to foot, from every pore, with blood and dirt'.

The pre-capitalist mode of production moved within 'narrow and more or less primitive bounds' and had to give way to new social and productive forces. Thus capitalism emerged, through the violent process of primitive accumulation, expropriating the small and scattered property of petty producers and divorcing them from their means of production. This process simultaneously created the wage workers on the one hand and the capitalists on the other, by concentrating the expropriated property in their hands as capital. The production process was transformed into one, which concentrates means of production, combines and socializes labour, experiences technological progress and connects itself with markets all over the world.

However, the advantages of this process of transformation have been cornered and appropriated by the capitalists, especially the business tycoons who emerge out of the centralization of capital. The workers are turned into a mass experiencing 'misery, oppression, slavery, degradation, exploitation'. Therefore, 'revolt' against this predicament also grows within the working class: 'a class always increasing in numbers, and disciplined, united, organized by the very mechanism of the process of capitalist production itself.' With monopoly ownership of capital increasingly becoming a fetter upon capitalist production, the revolt of the working class bursts the system of capitalist private property into pieces and expropriates the 'expropriators'.

This working class revolt against capitalist property does not recreate private property of the pre-capitalist era, but creates property based on 'the possession in common of the land and of the means of production.' Capitalist private property was created through the expropriation of the property of the masses by a few expropriators, through a violent and protracted process. The transformation of capitalist private property, which is already based on socialized production, into socialized property, is a far less difficult process of expropriating the property of a few capitalists by the masses.

CAPITAL: CONTEMPORARY RELEVANCE

One of the most abiding features of our social reality is the persistence of poverty among a large mass of people, despite the existence of abundant wealth and resources. The obvious reason behind this is the unequal distribution of income, wealth and resources in society. In fact, inequalities in income have grown in the advanced countries in the past three decades. An OECD report released in 2008 titled *Growing Unequal?*, after analysing the evidence of income distribution in 30 of its member countries, concludes:[6]

> The income of the richest 10% of people is, on average across OECD countries, nearly nine times that of the poorest 10% . . . the gap between rich and poor and the number of people below the poverty line have both grown over the past two decades. The increase is widespread, affecting three-quarters of OECD countries . . . income inequality increased significantly in the early 2000s in Canada, Germany, Norway and the United States . . .

This stark reality of capitalism today, springs out straight from the pages of *Capital*.

Before *Capital*, there were theories in political economy that explained why under capitalism, economies grow and wealth gets created on an expanding scale. There were also theories, which tried to explain, although with questionable accuracy, why poverty and inequality exist under capitalism. But it was in *Capital* that a theory was posited for the first time, which explained why growth and income inequality, wealth and poverty, coexist and get recursively reproduced under capitalism.

The proposition that poverty persists and inequality grows under capitalism, however, has been contested by many. They argue that increasing wealth created by capitalism gets shared with workers. So has wealth been shared with the workers under capitalism?

Persisting Poverty, Growing Inequality

The United States is the richest country in the world measured in terms of GDP. Here, the total number of people living below the official poverty line for individuals was 39.5 million (22% of population) in the late 1950s. This had declined to 23 million by the early 1970s (11%) but rose to 31 million by 2000 (11.3%). Since then it has gradually increased to 37 million in 2005 (12.6%), 39.8 million (13.2%) in 2008 and 43.6 million (14.3%) in 2009.[7] There is no single poverty line the US. Poverty estimates are done on the basis of different household income thresholds, depending on the number of family members and dependents in a household. If we take the weighted average poverty threshold for a family of four in 2009 as a benchmark, the poverty line in the US currently stands at around $15 per day (per head). The poverty line is a little less for households with higher family sizes, but even for the highest family size it would not be less than $13 per day (per head). There are over forty million people living below this poverty line in the US today, which is the largest number in the last fifty years.

The official minimum wage in the US in this decade was around $47 per day on average. Thus, those earning the minimum wage are excluded from the US poverty estimates. On the other hand, the average American CEO in 2007 earned more in one workday than what the average worker earned in the entire year (there are 260 workdays in a year). CEO pay rose on an average by 167% between 1989 to 2007, while the average nominal wage of the workers grew by only 10% during the same period. In the 1960s and 70s, CEOs in major American companies earned around 25 to 30 times more than an average worker; this ratio grew to almost 300 by the year 2000 and stood at around 275 in 2007.[8]

What is the social consequence of this? While the earnings of the bottom 90% of Americans grew by 15% between 1979 and 2006, that of the top 1% grew by 144% and the topmost 0.1% by 324%. Consequently, the earnings of the top 0.1% of US population in 2006 was 77 times the earnings of the bottom 90%; this was around 21 times in 1979.[9] Thus, while much of the world's wealth gets concentrated within the US as the world's richest country, this wealth gets further concentrated within a very narrow stratum of American society.

Capitalist Exploitation

Such a societal outcome follows from Marx's analysis in *Capital* that since capitalist production is based on class exploitation, the reproduction of capital, while creating much wealth under capitalism, also concentrates that wealth, reproduces poverty and widens income inequality. Persistence of poverty and rising inequality of income are natural corollaries of the property relations under capitalism, where the workers own nothing but their labour power, while the capitalists own everything else required for the production process. This enables the capitalists to extract surplus value from the workers in the production process and realise it as profits. What workers get as wages can never be more than a small fraction of the total value of their produce.

This concept of class exploitation under capitalism is of crucial importance, because capitalism survives by blurring this concept. What underlies the persistent poverty and growing inequality in the US and other rich countries is the exploitation of their workers by their capitalists. But this exploitation is concealed by getting the workers of the rich countries to look away from the yawning gap between their earnings and that of their business magnates, and to focus on the differences between their income and that of the workers of the poor countries. In other words, an American worker is reminded that while his/her minimum wage is $47 a day, 1.2 billion people across the world live on less than $1.25 a day.[10] But no one points out that an American CEO earns 275 times the American worker.

Thus, exploitation is made to disappear through this sleight of hand, by first introducing relativity in exploitation: you are not exploited because there are numerous others elsewhere whose exploitation is much more than yours. Then there is an implicit threat: if you still persist with efforts to end or reduce your exploitation, you will land up with those elsewhere who are more exploited. This tightly constrains the extent to which workers can reduce their exploitation by claiming and securing more wages. Even if the wages of workers increase from time to time, they increase so slowly that prices of everything else rise manifold compared to wages, pushing the real wage down. If we compare the average minimum wage of this decade with that of past decades, the real value of the US minimum wage (in 2007 dollars) fell from around $58 per day in the 1970s to $50 per day in the 1990s, and further to around $47 per day in the 2000s.[11]

Moreover, even as capitalist exploitation intensifies over time, the actual reason why a billion plus people earn less than $1.25 a day is also concealed from everyone. Those billion plus people are told that they are exploited because they do not earn $47 per day like the American workers, and development of capitalism over time will eventually increase their income to those levels.

Imperialist Exploitation

But what is the actual reason behind a billion plus people living below $1.25 a day? In order to understand that we have to extend the analytical framework of *Capital* — which is based on a closed capitalist system in a single country — into a world which is divided between rich and poor countries. There is a second tier of exploitation under capitalism, apart from the first tier of class exploitation. Capitalism came into being through the violent and gory process of 'primitive accumulation'; which involved expropriation of land and the destruction of domestic pre-capitalist producers like the peasants, artisans, weavers, etc., who became wage-workers under capitalism; and the expropriation of resources from across the world through colonial conquests, plunder, slave trade and slavery. Thus the initial development of capitalism itself, by exploiting the people, natural resources, minerals and other wealth of the colonies, led to the division of the world between the rich capitalist countries where wealth was concentrated and the poor countries whose populations were pauperized and robbed of their wealth.

Thus, colonialism created the second tier of exploitation under capitalism, and historically created a difference between the earnings of the wage workers in the rich countries and the pauperized masses in the colonies. The process of direct colonial rule continued till the middle of twentieth century, after which most of these poor countries attained national liberation. However, the end of colonial rule did not signify an end of the exploitation of the poor countries. Centuries of colonial rule created a world capitalist system where the big capitalist monopolies based in the rich countries owned and controlled much of capital and resources. Their imperialist domination of the world economy therefore continued and maintained the division of the world between rich and poor countries created by colonialism. Imperialist powers fought wars between them for further redivision of the poor countries, in order to extend the 'sphere of influence' for their respective monopoly capitalists and big banks (finance capital).[12]

Today, imperialism continues to function through the global domination of world production, trade and finance by monopoly capital; giant blocs of MNCs, banks and financial companies which can together be conceived as international finance capital; and the economic and military/strategic hegemony of the rich imperialist powers, led by the US. How does imperialist exploitation operate in today's world of globalized capitalism? It primarily operates through uneven development, which perpetuates the historical backwardness of the poor countries. The huge mass of people in the poor countries, who were pauperized through colonial exploitation, continue to exist today as a vast reserve of labour, who do not find gainful employment. The existence of this enormous reserve of labour — the unemployed, underemployed, informal wage workers and self-employed petty producers in the urban areas alongwith the peasants and landless agricultural workers in the rural areas — ensure that the wage or earning levels of bulk of the population in these poor countries remain tethered at bare subsistence levels. Imperialist exploitation operates through the perpetuation of this 'reserve labour' and manifests itself in the billion plus people in the world earning less than $1.25 a day.[13]

The class exploitation of the workers within the rich capitalist countries rests on the edifice of this imperialist exploitation. However, just as the class exploitation of the American workers is obfuscated by pointing to the wage differentials between the rich and poor countries, imperialist exploitation is obfuscated by rays of hope of the following kind, which are streamed in from the World Bank time to time:[14]

> Between 1981 and 2005, the share of the population in the developing world living below $1.25 a day was halved from 52 to 25 percent . . . reducing the number of poor by 500 million (from 1.9 billion to 1.4 billion) between 1981 and 2005.

But can the fact of 500 million more people increasing their earning over $1.25 a day, in a span of 24 years, be construed as a reduction of poverty?[15] Especially when a bulk of them continued to earn less than $2 a day. The same authors report that in these 24 years the number of people earning less than $2 a day remained *unchanged* at around 2.5 billion. It has remained unchanged because 'reserve labour' has persisted, signifying imperialist exploitation.

Moreover, if it takes 24 years, say, for 500 million poor people to increase their income from $1 a day to $2 a day, it will take at least another 264 years for them to reach the current minimum poverty line of the US at around $13 a day, and another 816 years to reach the $47 a day minimum wage level of the US. Broadly, this implies that at the current rate at which we are going, it will take nearly a thousand years for the 'reserve labour' of the poor countries to graduate from their present stage of imperialist exploitation to the stage of capitalist exploitation currently being experienced by the American workers. Moreover, would the minimum wage level in the US remain the same for the next thousand years? And if it does, what would it imply vis-à-vis the exploitation of the American workers?[16]

'Ending' Poverty?

Today's policymakers, however, are not bothered about these questions anymore. They keep themselves busy with the job of poverty 'reduction', embodied in the so-called Millennium Development Goals (MDGs), set by the United Nations in 2001 with the slogan, 'We Can End Poverty'. The latest stocktaking of the MDGs by the UN, however, is quite revealing.[17] It claims that the world is 'on track' to meet the MDG target of halving the proportion of people living on less than $1 a day between 1990 and 2015. Yet the numbers of those suffering from hunger *went up by 13 million* between 1990 and 2007. The effects of the economic crisis will push *an additional 64 million* people into extreme poverty in 2010. And *920 million people would continue living* under $1.25 a day in 2015. In effect, therefore, we are witnessing an increase in both poverty and hunger even as the world is supposedly 'on track' to meet the MDG target.

What nourishes this inane exercise is the mainstream academic discourse on poverty and inequality, which evades any serious analysis of the causes behind them and obsessively revolves around issues of definitions and measurements. Why is the international poverty line set at $1.25 per day? As per the World Bank's explanation, it is the average of poverty lines found in the 15 poorest countries. But what accounts for the average poverty line of 15 poorest countries being set at $1.25 per day? The rich and affluent sections in many of these countries earn several hundred times more than that. Yet, the bare subsistence level in the poorest countries is set as the standard for international poverty.

In the process, the distinction between capitalist and imperialist exploitation gets blurred and the value of labour gets universally degraded. And even after defining poverty in such an ideological manner, poverty alleviation targets are not being met in most countries. Just imagine the consequence of the entire poverty discourse, if the American poverty line of $30 per day is made the international poverty line.

Two Ideas of Justice

The basic problem with the concepts of poverty being used by the World Bank or the UN today, however, lies in its underlying notion of justice. Adam Smith, who authored one of the most celebrated of treatises in political economy, *The Wealth of Nations* (1776) — which justifies the individual self-interest driven order under capitalism because it creates wealth and leads to greater social good — also wrote *The Theory of Moral Sentiments* (1759), which termed the disposition to 'despise' or 'neglect' of poor persons as a 'corruption of our moral sentiments' and forcefully urged for more 'sympathy'.[18] Yet, Marx criticized Adam Smith's views as that of a *'fatalist'* economist; who looks at poverty merely as a birthpang of capitalism and not as one which gets reproduced alongwith wealth under capitalism; and who thereby remains 'indifferent' towards the 'sufferings of the proletarians'.[19] These divergent views on poverty arise out of two notions of social justice, which need to be contradistinguished.

Underlying Adam Smith's views on poverty is an apologetic notion of justice, based on the categories of 'neglect', 'despise', 'sympathy' and 'moral sentiments'. If we try to develop these implicit notions of injustice and justice into explicit social objectives, the former would require an *a priori* identification of the aspects of 'neglect' of the poor, on whose removal the social effort needs to be channelized. The problem is that categories like 'neglect' are purely subjective and have no benchmark. What comprises 'neglect' would always vary, both across time and societies. Therefore, what is realizable as justice would forever remain loosely defined. And within this loosely defined framework of justice, it can never be concluded, whether justice is being or not being done. Needless to say, it is this framework of justice that drives the World Bank poverty estimates and the UN MDGs today.

To this complacent moral universe of justice as apology, *Capital* delivers an electric shock. Its superiority arises from the fact that by rigorously establishing the category of exploitation as ensconced in the production process, it provides a firm anchor to social justice. It drags the idea of justice out from the sphere of morality and ethics into the material sphere of production, distribution and ownership of wealth. Thus defined, the attainment of ultimate justice becomes the end of exploitation. Whether a society is more or less just, or moving towards more or less justice, can also be judged on the basis of whether there is more or less exploitation. In other words, the goalposts of justice cannot be shifted.

It is argued by some that this clarity in its notion of justice is also the main weakness of *Capital*, because by taking a maximalist position — end exploitation to end poverty — it actually fails to achieve either, because ending exploitation entails a radical revolution against capitalist property. Since the revolution either happens or it doesn't, there is nothing to do in between. This confusion arises from a misreading of *Capital*.

What *Capital* does is to historicize exploitation under capitalism, by tracing its origins through the process of 'primitive' accumulation into the evolution of modern industrial capitalism. This demystification of the exploitation process enables concrete praxis on the part of the exploited against their exploitation, on the one hand, and universalizes that praxis, on the other. Within its framework of justice, a whole body of socio-economic rights can be clearly conceived, struggled for and actualized over time, signifying progress towards ultimate justice.

This framework of justice, moreover, suggests that efforts to stabilize and ameliorate exploitation under capitalism through policy interventions can succeed only if struggles against exploitation simultaneously persist alongside those efforts, in order to ensure progress towards ultimate justice. In the absence of those struggles or in the case of their gradual decay, exploitation will once again intensify under the spontaneous tendencies of capitalism, snatching away extant rights and entitlements. The struggle against exploitation therefore becomes the bulwark of justice for the poor under capitalism.

There are of course serious forms of oppression and inequities which exist in society that are distinct from class exploitation — based on gender, caste, race, language or ethnicity. While *Capital* does not deal with such injustices independently, what it does and uniquely so, is not to limit the notion of social justice within the bounds of exploitative property and production relations. This idea of justice creates space for the poor, cutting across gender, caste, race, language or ethnicity, to come together to struggle against their class exploitation, advance their rights and make progress towards a society free from such exploitation. It is the weakening of such struggles today — locally and globally, both on the ground and in the realm of ideas — which has not just made the discourse on justice poorer but also robbed the discourse on poverty of all substance and vitality. *Capital's* contemporary relevance therefore lies in resuscitating such struggles.

IMPERIALIST GLOBALIZATION

Let us look at the process of globalization on the basis of the concepts we have built so far. The process is essentially imperialist because it enables international finance capital to globalize capitalist exploitation without upsetting the bulwark of imperialist exploitation, based on perpetuating 'reserve labour'. Compared to the earlier phase of twentieth century imperialism, the globalization process, which can roughly be dated back to the 1970s, has led to the shifting of manufacturing processes and service based economic activities into the poor countries. This has changed the earlier pattern of international division of labour. However, the diffusion of capitalist development in the poor countries has not led to a universalization of capitalist exploitation. It has rather created enclaves of capitalist exploitation, ensconced within the overall landscape of imperialist exploitation.

Globalized Exploitation
This pattern of capitalist development has led to an intensification of both forms of exploitation. Those suffering from capitalist exploitation still consider themselves to be relatively fortunate in escaping imperialist exploitation. Therefore they submit to the whims and fancies of capital, staying away from trade unions, even accepting to work below minimum wages for longer working hours and undergo many more travails, just to ensure that they are not thrown out of the enclave of capitalist exploitation into the landscape of imperialist exploitation. This not only tethers the minimum wages in the poor countries to very low levels, but the mobility of capital under globalization, from the rich to the poor countries also create downward pressure on the wages in the rich countries. What capital mobility does therefore is to enable capital to use the 'reserve labour' of the poor countries, to weaken the bargaining strength of the workers everywhere, both in the poor as well as the rich countries. The outcome is seen in the

'flexibilization' of labour across the rich and poor countries, throwing to the winds all labour legislation — *de jure* or *de facto* — degrading capitalist exploitation further. It is also snatching away the hard won rights of the international working class movement of the past century.

As far as those suffering from imperialist exploitation are concerned, the carrot of 'including' them into the enclaves of capitalist exploitation is dangled in myriad forms. But the capitalist enclaves in the poor countries; because of the very global nature of their demand patterns, technologies, labour processes, skill requirements and financial networks; do not absorb sufficient labour from the surrounding world of 'reserve labour'. Moreover, their backward and forward linkages are principally with the rich countries and similar capitalist enclaves in other poor countries, and not with the pre-capitalist landscape where they are ensconced. Rather than diffusing economic activities onto the pre-capitalist landscape, they remain as restricted enclaves of capitalist production. Therefore 'reserve labour' persists. In fact, in a replay of colonial exploitation, they are often dispossessed of their petty or common properties in land and forests in order to make way for those enclaves of capitalist exploitation. This 'primitive' accumulation continues alongside capitalist and imperialist exploitation.

But why does capitalist exploitation remain restricted within enclaves and not get universalised over time? What accounts for the perpetuation of 'reserve labour' and imperialist exploitation in the long run? It is because capitalism, even in its globalized avatar, ultimately remains a crisis-ridden system incapable of continued expanded reproduction. Periodic crises, which inevitably recur under capitalism, destroy capital and constrain its productive forces. This makes it systemically incapable of absorbing the 'reserve labour' by providing it with gainful employment.

Capitalism and Crisis
Capital's analysis locates the crisis tendencies of capitalism at the very heart of its accumulation process. Wealth created under capitalism largely accrues to capitalists as higher profits. This is ensured through the nature of technological progress itself, whereby labour productivity rises continuously, restraining employment growth. As a result, the 'reserve army' of the unemployed persists, preventing the workers from increasing their wages and securing a better share in the social produce. These limits on the share of the workers in the social produce also limits their purchasing power, thereby

limiting the growth of the market. This makes the system prone to crises, characterized by periodic over-production of commodities, which capitalists are unable to sell.

A crisis occurs when the reproduction process hits the limits of the market. Unsold commodities accumulate and profits dry up, making the capitalists unwilling to employ their capital. The entire accumulation process gets disrupted, resulting in closure of enterprises and destruction of capital on the one hand and the swelling of the 'reserve army' of unemployed on the other.

It is often argued that Keynes also theorized this in *The General Theory of Employment, Interest and Money* (1936) by analyzing how deficiency of aggregate demand can create deep recessions under capitalism. It is true that *General Theory* argued against cutting wages during recessions and advocated state intervention in demand management to reduce unemployment. But it did so more as an inside critique to fix the deficiencies of capitalism in the short-run. The strength of *General Theory* lies in its rich analysis of the speculative motive, liquidity preference and 'animal spirits', which is essential to understand the sharp fluctuations under capitalism in today's age of globalized finance. However, *Capital*'s analysis of accumulation and crisis under capitalism is at a different plane. That difference is best understood in today's world of globalized production and finance.

The theory of employment and unemployment contained in *General Theory* is a short period one. The phenomenon of jobless growth witnessed under globalization is therefore something which the *General Theory* would not be able to adequately explain. *Capital*, however, looks at technological progress — increasing automation of production — as a means of displacing labour by capital in order to maintain the reserve army of unemployed. Unemployment plays a functional role here, in enhancing the power of capital over labour, keeping it under strict discipline and restraining wage growth. An under-consumptionist tendency is built into the very nature of technological progress under capitalism. Therefore, restricted consumption of the working masses is the basic underlying cause of crisis under capitalism.

For technological progress to occur under capitalism without increasing unemployment, ever-expanding investment by the state is required. Moreover, the level of investment by the state in labour absorbing activities, must be so high as to generate sufficient employment growth which compensates for the growth of productivity in capital-intensive sectors. The pace of introduction of labour displacing technology and their diffusion also needs to be regulated by the state.

Under globalization though, neither of the conditions has worked, because the essence of the globalization process has been the unleashing of the spontaneous tendencies of capital, free from any encumbrances of the state. The growing disconnect between investment and output growth on the one hand and employment and wages on the other — jobless growth and squeeze in real wages — is a direct consequence of this. It is the aggravation of the under-consumptionist tendency under globalization, arising out of jobless growth and depressed wages on account of intensified capitalist exploitation, which set the stage for a global economic crisis, which finally erupted in 2008.[20]

Resurgence of Money-Capital

Nobody expected the British monarch, a relic of its pre-capitalist past, to crack one of the darkest jokes of the modern era, by asking academics at the London School of Economics in November 2008 why they did not 'notice' the coming of the global financial crisis. It is not as surreal as it appears though, given that Her Majesty's personal investment portfolio is valued at £100 million, which may have shrunk a bit in that 'awful' mess. The academics later explained the 'psychology of denial' in a letter by stating that the crisis was a result of a failure to understand 'risks to the system as a whole'. The solution offered is to develop 'horizon-scanning capability' so that the 'forecasting-failure' occurs 'never again'.[21]

As far as 'horizon-scanning capability' is concerned, *Capital* does not have any theory on the state of expectations or liquidity preference, which mark the originality of *General Theory*. But it does contain an elaborate discussion on 'money-capital' (finance) and 'real capital', which provides deep insights into the development of the financial sphere of capitalism, its inter-relationship with the accumulation process and its role in aggravating the crisis tendencies of capitalism. This helps us to better assess the 'risks to the system as a whole'.

Superimposed on the capital accumulation process, characterized by an under-consumptionist tendency, is the credit and financial system, which by making money owned by others available to capitalists, enables extended reproduction and centralization of capital. Centralization eventually creates a 'superabundance' of 'money-capital', which expresses itself in a 'plethora' of forms other than cash, like stocks, bonds and mortgages, whose transactions as commodities lead to the creation of 'illusory' value. This becomes 'more and more a matter of gamble', which attracts more and more of money-capital into these transactions. This causes sharp inflation in asset prices, which artificially causes a 'forced expansion' of the reproduction process. When these artificially inflated prices eventually crash, there is a rush to sell financial assets and 'only cash payments have validity'. This causes credit to dry up because money-capitalists become unwilling to lend, and as a result the reproduction process gets disrupted, precipitating crises in both the spheres of financial and real capital.

At least three important conclusions follow from this in the context of globalization. First, 'euthanasia of the rentier' as prescribed by the *General Theory* becomes a far-fetched idea under capitalism, because while 'money-capital' and 'real capital' can be conceptually segregated with ease, they exist in the real world as a bloc deeply intertwined with each other. Even if the excesses of 'money-capital' can be curbed through state regulation for a while, the spontaneous tendency of centralization of real capital would inevitably bring 'money-capital' back in action through its 'superabundance'.

Second, 'socialization of investment' naturally becomes a less preferable option for capitalism in a world where a 'forced expansion' of the reproduction process can be caused, however temporarily, through inflation in asset prices. Debt-driven consumption bubbles of the rich and affluent take the place of workers' consumption as the driver of economic activity.

Third, in a world where 'money-capital' corners an increasing share of surplus-value by creating 'illusory' value, through the movement in asset prices independent of real capital — and that too across national boundaries — 'approximation to full employment' is bound to be abandoned as state policy. This is because international finance capital requires the stability of the international monetary system, for its own smooth functioning. This stability in the value of money (across currencies) is provided by stabilizing money wages, both through 'flexibilization' of labour as well as the maintenance of 'reserve labour'.

The atrophy of social democracy as an economic philosophy within the rich countries and the ascendancy of neoliberalism follow from these developments, which have unfolded in the capitalist world since the 1970s. After being regulated and controlled by the state during the post-war decades of Keynesian demand management, money-capital witnessed resurgence in the shape of international finance capital. The results — in terms of increasing poverty and income inequality across the world, declining real wages, concentration of capital on an unprecedented scale, its cross-border mobility, skyrocketing CEO pay, financial deregulation, asset price bubbles, sub-prime lending — and all this eventually leading to the financial meltdown and great recession of 2008/2009; are there for everyone to see.

What is more revealing is the rapidity with which the 'we-are-all-Keynesians-now' mood of the immediate aftermath of the crisis has evaporated within the capitalist policy establishments, giving way to the same neoliberal humbug and hubris that caused the crisis in the first place. After spending humongous amounts of taxpayers' money to bail out the failed investment banks and mortgage lenders, the policy locus in the rich countries has shifted back to the orthodoxy of cutting deficits and imposing austerity.

While the IMF and the World Bank had forecast a revival of the global economy in 2010, the latest assessment by the OECD cautions of a 'slowdown in the pace of recovery' in the second half of 2010.[22] This slowdown of growth is taking place at a time when unemployment rates are ranging between 9.5 to 10 per cent in the US and Europe. OECD's *Employment Outlook 2010* released in July 2010 reports 47 million people to be officially unemployed in OECD countries, with 17 million more people out of work from the beginning of the crisis in 2007. It further states that taking into account those who have given up looking for work or are working part-time but want to work full-time, the actual number of unemployed and under-employed in OECD countries could be about 80 million.

The pursuit of austerity measures by the governments of the rich countries, even in the backdrop of such historically high levels of unemployment, demonstrates the continued hegemony of international finance capital. While the *General Theory* would certainly be upset by such a predicament, which goes totally against its analysis and policy prescriptions, the strength of *Capital* lies in its capacity to explain why matters have come to such a pass.

FREEDOM AND REVOLUTION

Any crisis of capitalism inevitably conjures specters of the collapse of capitalism. The ongoing crisis of the capitalist world has been no exception. Is this the end of capitalism that Marx had predicted? However, this notion of capitalism as a system collapsing after hitting the dead-end of an economic crisis finds no place in the analysis of *Capital*. It shows capitalism to be a system which contains spontaneous and contradictory tendencies of expansion and crisis, and which moves in time through these contradictory processes. It gets out of a mess only to land up, as the Queen might say, in another 'awful' one. The spate of debt, currency and financial crises the capitalist world has witnessed since the 1980s, eventually leading to the grand financial meltdown in the US in 2008 and the ongoing 'great recession', exposes that crisis-ridden character of capitalism. It is incapable of any sustained process of expansion. There are limits.

Revolutionary Framework

There is, however, a story about the end of capitalism in *Capital*, the story of proletarian revolution. Just as capitalism was born out of a revolution against feudalism, it will come to an end through a revolution by the workers against monopoly capital. While proletarian revolutions have not occurred in the rich capitalist countries till date, the first revolution inspired by Marx's ideas happened in Russia.[23] China and several other poor countries followed suit, which demonstrated the power of Marx's concepts and analytical framework. Those revolutions were not 'pure' proletarian revolutions as was envisaged in *Capital* but were based upon innovations in both theory and praxis by revolutionary leaders like Lenin and Mao. But the starting point of all revolutionary theory since Marx has remained his framework.

The strength of the Marxian framework, as can be seen in *Capital*, lies in the fact that it does not look at capitalism as an ossified structure frozen in time but as a set of relationships and processes moving over time. Moreover, the framework is also adaptable, in the sense that insightful theories and objective analyses of society developed independently can also gel together with this framework, to enrich the analysis of the relationships and processes under capitalism. In other words, Marxism is and was always intended to be a scientific and revolutionary framework and not a set of religious beliefs or dogmas that claim to contain every truth about the world within its texts.

Under the present stage of imperialist globalization, the possibility of a 'pure' proletarian revolution in a rich capitalist country continues to look distant. It is the world of poor countries, which always remains alive with the possibility of revolution, because this world is home to the most exploited sections of humanity. The anti-imperialist upsurge in Latin America witnessed over the past decade has shown the future direction for the revolutionary struggles in the poor countries. Much of the innovations in theory and praxis introduced by Lenin and Mao, also continue to remain relevant in the context of imperialism, especially the concept of a democratic revolution based on worker-peasant alliance against imperialism and monopoly capital.

Workers and 'Reserve Labour'

What our analysis of imperialist globalization suggests, though, is the importance of bringing the classes comprising 'reserve labour' in the poor countries, to the centre stage of political and revolutionary mobilization. These are the peasantry and rural labourers on the one hand and the unemployed, underemployed, informal wage workers and self-employed petty producers in the urban areas on the other. These classes within the poor countries are bearing the brunt of imperialist exploitation today, living a life of drudgery, insecurity and impoverishment, in the swamp of the informal sector.

They helplessly watch the cruel joke being played on them by the national and international policy establishments, in the name of 'poverty reduction', 'inclusive growth', 'MDGs' and so on, even as rising prices of food and fuel eat away the pittance that they make after a very hard day's work. And even those low paying jobs have been snatched away from many of them by the economic crisis. These are the two billion plus who yearn the most for freedom from their exploitation.

The unity between the workers facing capitalist exploitation and the 'reserve labour' facing imperialist exploitation is the key. The intensification of capitalist exploitation cannot be fought back without fighting imperialist exploitation, which perpetuates 'reserve labour'. Marx while discussing the role of the reserve army of the unemployed in *Capital* had noted that their existence and recreation enables the 'despotism' of capital. This acquires added significance in today's world of globalized capital, where the 'disciplined, united, organized' workforce envisaged in *Capital* has increasingly given way to a multitude of casualized and irregular workers.

The structure of the capitalist production process itself has changed with decentralization, sub-contracting and outsourcing of work, which have led to an overwhelmingly unorganized working class, considerably blurring the distinction between the employed and the unemployed. In this context, the suggestion made in *Capital* for workers and their trade unions 'to organize a regular co-operation between employed and unemployed in order to destroy or to weaken the ruinous effects of this natural law of capitalistic production on their class', acquires significance.

It is on the bedrock of this revolutionary alliance between workers and 'reserve labour', against imperialism and the domestic ruling classes that the next tide of revolutionary transformations in this century has to be based.

NOTES

1 The first volume of *Capital* was published during Marx's lifetime in 1867. After his death in 1883, the second and third volumes were published in 1885 and 1894 respectively, by Marx's lifelong friend and collaborator, Friedrich Engels.

2 "Preface to *Capital* Volume One", in Louis Althusser, *Lenin and Philosophy and Other Essays*, Monthly Review Press, 2001.

3 Marx's Eleventh Thesis on Feuerbach.

4 Marx apologized in advance for the difficulty that readers would encounter in following the very first chapter of the book: 'Every beginning is difficult, holds in all sciences. To understand the first chapter, especially the section that contains the analysis of commodities, will, therefore, present the greatest difficulty.' See 'Preface to the First German Edition', *Capital*, I.

5 The value of a piece of wood comes from the labour applied to cut it from the tree. The value of a chair made from that piece of wood comes from the labour applied to design and make the chair.

6 *Growing Unequal? Income Distribution and Poverty in OECD Countries*, Organization for Economic Co-operation and Development, Paris, 2008. The OECD is a club of advanced capitalist countries, which currently has 33 members.

7 Data sourced from the website of Institute for Research on Poverty, University of Wisconsin-Madison. Primary source of data is the US Census Bureau. The poverty estimation methodology has been revised in the US four times since the 1950s, the last time being 1981.

8 See Figure 3AE in Chapter 3 on *Wages* in *The State of Working America 2008/ 2009*.

9 Ibid.

10 *Poverty: Recent Estimates and Outlook*, World Bank website, (updated March 2010).

11 Table 3.38 in Lawrence Mishel, Jared Bernstein and Heidi Shierholz, *The State of Working America 2008/2009*, Economic Policy Institute, New York, 2009. Economist Robert Pollin has also shown on the basis of long period data that average real wages in the US peaked at $15.7 per hour in 1973 and fell since then to reach $14.13 per hour in 2000. The fall in average real wages

since the 1970s occurred despite continued growth in labour productivity. See his *Contours of Descent: US Economic Fractures and the Landscape of Global Austerity*, Verso Books, 2005.

12 For more on this see V.I. Lenin, *Imperialism: The Highest Stage of Capitalism*, with an Introduction by Prabhat Patnaik, LeftWord Books, New Delhi, 2000.

13 This is based on the theoretical framework developed by Prabhat Patnaik in *Accumulation and Stability Under Capitalism*, Clarendon Press Oxford, 1997. Patnaik identified these labour reserves in the poor countries as the ultimate shock absorbers of the world capitalist system, which provides it stability. He further develops this in Chapters 18 and 20 of *The Value of Money*, Tulika, New Delhi, 2009. The category of 'reserve labour' is conceptually different from the 'reserve army of labour' in *Capital*, which basically implies the unemployed under capitalism. In our extended framework, a person can belong to 'reserve labour' even when she is informally employed.

14 Data is based on Shaohua Chen and Martin Ravallion, 2008, 'The developing world is poorer than we thought, but no less successful in the fight against poverty', Policy Research Working Paper 4703, World Bank, 2008.

15 These international estimates of poverty are based on Purchasing Power Parity (PPP), i.e., they are corrected for inter-country variations in inflation and exchange rates. Estimates in terms of nominal earnings and exchange rates may show much higher levels of poverty. The following argument, however, is not based on this methodological aspect.

16 In fact, the federal minimum wage in the US has been increased in recent years and stands at around $58 per day since 2009. We continue to cite the decadal average of $47 per day for the sake of continuity with earlier arguments.

17 MDG Report, *United Nations*, 2010.

18 Adam Smith, *The Theory of Moral Sentiments*, Part I, Section III, Chapter III, 1759.

19 Karl Marx, *The Poverty of Philosophy*, "The Method", 1847.

20 For a detailed account of the financial crisis in the US, see Prasenjit Bose and Rohit (2008), 'Global Financial Crisis: Lessons in Theory and Policy', *The Marxist*, Volume XXIV, No. 3.

21 The text of the letter written by two members of the British Academy is available at: http://media.ft.com/cms/3e3b6ca8-7a08-11de-b86f-00144feabdc0.pdf

22 'What is the economic outlook for OECD countries? An Interim Assessment', Organization for Economic Co-operation and Development, Paris, September 2010.

23 Interestingly, Eric Hobsbawm notes that while the first German edition of *Capital* (thousand copies) published in 1867 took five years to sell out, thousand copies of the first Russian edition of 1872 sold out in less than two months. See his *The Age of Capital 1848-1875*, Abacus, 1975, p.308.

Reading Marx on Technology

T. Jayaraman

Marx's writing on technology, particularly in *Capital*, is profoundly significant. In an era where the question of technology is still the subject of much confusion in theory and practice, especially in the context of developing societies, his perspectives and insights on this subject are still among the deepest and most powerful.

The first striking aspect of Marx's views on technology is that he is one of the few thinkers whose conceptual and theoretical considerations on technology are consistently dialectical.

Marx had, following from his view of history, a keen appreciation of scientific and technological advances. Nowhere perhaps is this more tellingly illustrated than in Engels's speech at the graveside of Marx.[1] As Engels noted: 'Science was for Marx a historically dynamic, revolutionary force. However great the joy with which he welcomed a new discovery in some theoretical science whose practical application perhaps it was as yet quite impossible to envisage, he experienced quite another kind of joy when the discovery involved immediate revolutionary changes in industry, and in historical development in general.'[2]

It is significant that Marx's appreciation, in Engels' view, is not simply restricted to science as explanation or critique or understanding, but extends to technology. Secondly, Marx's enthusiasm for technology did not refer to technology in the future but included the radical advances made by technology even under contemporary capitalism.

At the same time, when it came to the impact of machinery on the lives and well-being of the working people under capitalism, Marx and Engels were unsparing in their critique.

Speaking on the impact of technology at the General Council meeting of the International Working Men's Association, Marx noted: '. . . what strikes us most is that all the consequences which were expected as the inevitable result of machinery have been reversed.'[3] He then refers to the increased exploitation that was the direct result of the introduction of machinery, and to the exploitation of women and children compelled to work brutally longer hours. He also pointed out that the labourer who owned his tools in an earlier era and was to an extent a free agent was transformed under capitalism, into 'a slave of capital in the capitalist factory.' He made the point that 'The influence of machinery upon those with whose labour it enters into competition is directly hostile. Many hand-loom weavers were positively killed by the introduction of the power-loom, both here and in India.' Marx concluded his speech, summarizing: 'To conclude for the present, machinery leads on the one hand to associated organized labour, on the other to the disintegration of all formerly existing social and family relations.' Note the dialectical treatment here, reminding us that even as machinery under capitalism leads to the disintegration of the worker's old world, it has the potential to lead to 'associated organized labour'.

THE NATURE OF TECHNOLOGY AS PRACTICE

The crucial point in Marx's analysis lies in his showing how the contradictory consequences of technological advance under capitalism have the same origin. How is this to be demonstrated?

The first volume of *Capital* is a brilliant scientific account of how this is to be done. *Capital* has a tight, logical structure, where Marx begins with the analysis of commodity production and the nature of value and moves on to the specific features of commodity production under capitalism, namely, labour power itself becoming a commodity and the production of surplus value. Following this, analysing the passage of this system of production through the stage of manufacture, Marx begins to uncover the nature of technology under capitalism.[4]

In the process, Marx offers some brilliant insights into the foundational aspect of technology in human society.

For Marx, knowledge is constituted by both theory and practice. In relation to the natural world, it is labour and later technology that is essentially practice. And it is the human species' constant activity, that transforms Nature (and in the process, the species), that drives the evolution of human society. As Marx puts it: 'Labour is, in the first place, a process in which both man and Nature participate, and in which man of his own accord starts, regulates, and controls the material reactions between himself and Nature. He opposes himself to Nature as one of her own forces, setting in motion arms and legs, head and hands, the natural forces of his body, in order to appropriate Nature's productions in a form adapted to his own wants. By thus acting on the external world and changing it, he at the same time changes his own nature' (*Capital*, I, p. 173).[5]

But the matter does not end here. In a brief but profound passage that follows the previous quotation, Marx delineates what is special about human labour: 'We pre-suppose labour in a form that stamps it as exclusively human. A spider conducts operations that resemble those of a weaver, and a bee puts to shame many an architect in the construction of her cells. But what distinguishes the worst architect from the best of bees is this, that the architect raises his structure in imagination before he erects it in reality. At the end of every labour-process, we get a result that already existed in the imagination of the labourer at its commencement. He not only effects a change of form in the material on which he works, but he also realises a purpose of his own that gives the law to his modus operandi, and to which he must subordinate his will' (*Capital*, I, p. 174).

Thus practice, in the form of labour, is not simply action, but conscious, purposive action, that erects the end result in imagination before seeking its realisation in the real world. I believe that it would not be incorrect to say that few commentators on Marx, even among Marxists, have explored the significance of this conception of practice and its link with theoretical understanding.[6]

How then does this view of human labour tie up with the 'revolution in the instruments of labour' that characterises modern industry? Marx offers this brilliant insight:

A critical history of technology would show how little any of the inventions of the 18th century are the work of a single individual. Hitherto there is no such book. Darwin has interested us in the history of Nature's Technology, i.e., in the formation of the organs of plants and animals, which organs serve as instruments of production for sustaining life. Does not the history of the productive organs of man, of organs that are the material basis of all social organisation, deserve equal attention? And would not such a history be easier to compile, since, as Vico says, human history differs from natural history in this, that we have made the former, but not the latter? Technology discloses man's mode of dealing with Nature, the process of production by which he sustains his life, and thereby also lays bare the mode of formation of his social relations, and of the mental conceptions that flow from them. Every history of religion, even, that fails to take account of this material basis, is uncritical. It is, in reality, much easier to discover by analysis the earthly core of the misty creations of religion, than, conversely, it is, to develop from the actual relations of life the corresponding celestialised forms of those relations. The latter method is the only materialistic, and therefore the only scientific one. The weak points in the abstract materialism of natural science, a materialism that excludes history and its process, are at once evident from the abstract and ideological conceptions of its spokesmen, whenever they venture beyond the bounds of their own speciality. (*Capital*, I, Ch. 15, n. 4, p. 352)

Quite apart from the many rich layers of meaning in these remarks, and the various directions for exploration that they open up, it is clear that, for Marx, technology is an extension of the productive organs of the human body, and is in essence, as plain human labour was at an earlier stage, part and parcel of man's mode of dealing with Nature. Thus Marx rids the question of technology of any mysticism; there is no question of counterposing technology to any human 'essence', as much of a long line of critique of capitalism that begins with European Romanticism is wont to do.

Technology therefore is integral to the nature of humans as part of the specific nature of their existence as a species, and the specific form that the evolution of this particular species has taken subsequently. As the historian Hobsbawm remarks in a recent essay, the evolution of human society represents a move from the purely genetic to 'accelerating inheritance of acquired characteristics through cultural rather than genetic mechansims.'[7] Hobsbawm notes further: 'History is the continuation of the biological evolution of the species by other means.' He draws out the following implication:

It inevitably returns us to the basic approach to human evolution adopted by archaeologists and prehistorians, which is to study the modes of interaction between our species and its environment and its growing control over it. That means asking the questions that Marx asked. 'Modes of production' (or whatever we want to call them), based on major innovations in productive technology, in communications, and in social organisation—but also in military power—have been central to human evolution. These innovations, as

Marx was aware, did not and do not make themselves. Material and cultural forces and relations of production are not separable. They are the activities of men and women in historical situations not of their making, acting and taking decisions ('making their history'), but not in a vacuum—not even a vacuum of imputed rational calculation.

THE TECHNOLOGICAL REVOLUTION AND THE MACHINE

Among the enduring legacies of Marx's study of human society is the understanding that all categories relating to human society must be understood in their historical context. Thus even while Marx begins with underlining the broad continuity between human labour and technology, in that both relate to the interaction of humans with Nature, he also emphasises the study of the particular features of technology under capitalism, features that mark and set off the nature of the forces of production under capitalism from the forces of production in pre-capitalist society.

What turns technology, that is a product of human labour, into an external, alien force that comes to rule over labour itself?[8] From Marx's viewpoint of historical materialism, the first task is to understand how the transformation of the relations of production of pre-capitalist society paves the way for the revolutionary transformation of the instruments of labour. The second task is to study the specific forms of the development of productive forces that ensue with the establishment of capitalism. The first stage, as Marx notes, is in manufacture, where 'the revolution in the mode of production begins with labour power.' Manufacture itself leads to a jump in productivity, with the transformation of the way in which production is organised. In manufacture, masses of workers are gathered together under one roof, and the task of each one is broken down into some basic element of the series of actions that go into the making of a particular artefact. At the same time, manufacturing also brings under one roof all the elements of producing goods that were produced by different classes of craftsmen and artisans in separate locations. Manufacturing sets the stage for the technological revolution but does so specifically in the manner of the use of labour power and its organisation. But at this stage there is as yet no radical transformation of the tools that are used.

Manufacture is an age of ever-increasing and brutal exploitation. But, as the physical limits of such exploitation are reached, even as capitalism demands ever-increasing production and as working class resistance to this grows, the stage is set for the next phase of the development of the forces of production, namely the introduction of machinery. Thus Marx notes the origins of the technological drive of capitalism: 'At last the critical point was reached. The basis of the old method, sheer brutality in the exploitation of the workpeople, accompanied more or less by a systematic division of labour, no longer sufficed for the extending markets and for the still more rapidly extending competition of the capitalists. The hour struck for the advent of machinery.'

The chapter on machinery in *Capital*, I, counts among the most powerfully written parts of Marx's greatest work. Marx begins with a study of the machine and underlines the quantum jump that the machine represents in contrast to human labour. The machine, in Marx's analysis, is the concrete and basic unit of the technological revolution and it is the further development of machinery and its spread and evolution that leads to the second revolution in the mode of production, namely 'the revolution in the instruments of labour'. But even as machinery replaces the imprecise human hand, by increased precision, quality and speed of operation, and overall shortens the time required to produce a given commodity, signalling the enormous growth in the human ability to produce material goods, the contradictory aspect of machinery immediately comes into view. Despite its promise, the effect of machinery is an opposite one on the life of the workers in the branch of industry where it has affected entry. It increases the length of the working day. However, both by virtue of the physical limitations of long hours of labour and the rising resistance of the working class, legal limits on length of the working day emerge, even as capital responds by the intensification of labour, and where possible, violation of laws.

Marx is no technological determinist. For him, the level of technological development is characteristic of a particular stage of the evolution of human society, not as the cause but as an indicator. Thus manufacture precedes the era of modern industry, and capitalist relations of production are established before machinery enters the scene. Machinery is irself an outcome of the class struggle between labour and capital and of competition among capitalists.

Let us turn now to Marx's account of the manner in which machinery rationalises the process of production:

Modern Industry rent the veil that concealed from men their own social process of production, and that turned the various, spontaneously divided branches of production into so many riddles, not only to outsiders, but even to the initiated. The principle which it pursued, of resolving each process into its constituent movements, without any regard to their possible execution by the hand of man, created the new modern science of technology. The varied, apparently unconnected, and petrified forms of the industrial processes now resolved themselves into so many conscious and systematic applications of natural science to the attainment of given useful effects. Technology also discovered the few main fundamental forms of motion, which, despite the diversity of the instruments used, are necessarily taken by every productive action of the human body; just as the science of mechanics sees in the most complicated machinery nothing but the continual repetition of the simple mechanical powers. (*Capital*, I, Ch. 15, pp. 456–57)

A striking feature of this passage is that it could well apply today to the labour process of sections of what are known as the knowledge economy. Computer software and algorithms serve to do for mental labour in the form of mathematical operations what the machine did for manual labour. Though, as Marx remarks, in the era of mechanization, science is separated from the worker, a separation that is also a condition indispensable for the growth of the former, it is nevertheless true that in the modern era when scientific work is directly related to the production process, scientific work undergoes the same processes that befell manual labour more than a century ago. Machinery has invaded also the chemical and biological laboratories and automation and robotics have replaced the hand of the technician with machines that have several times higher and more accurate throughput per unit of time.

Throughout the capitalist era, even after Marx's time, capitalists have always sought to intensify the labour process, speeding it up, introducing new machinery, etc.[9] A typical example of this historically was the introduction of techniques of managing the production process that came to be referred to collectively as Taylorism and/or Fordism. An integral part of this development was the widespread use of assembly lines in manufacturing. Another important part of these new techniques were time and motion studies that began an era of rationalising and making more accurate whatever remained of the human hand in the labour process. The era of the assembly line is by no means over, even though the elementary units of the assembly line have undergone substantial changes. The introduction of computers, automation and robotics have radically changed the nature of both machines themselves and the assembly lines in many industries. Nevertheless, it is clear that such changes in production techniques do not represent any qualitative change in the mode of production but constitute part of the relentless drive for the intensification of the production process and labour under capitalism. Thus, even as technology advances, every advance brings alongside intensification of labour.[10]

Marx repeatedly draws attention to the revolutionary implications of the introduction of machinery, particularly after industry reaches the stage of producing machines through machines. 'Modern Industry never looks upon and treats the existing form of a process as final. The technical basis of that industry is therefore revolutionary, while all earlier modes of production were essentially conservative. By means of machinery, chemical processes and other methods, it is continually causing changes not only in the technical basis of production, but also in the functions of the labourer, and in the social combinations of the labour-process. At the same time, it thereby also revolutionises the division of labour within the society, and incessantly launches masses of capital and of workpeople from one branch of production to another' (*Capital*, I, p. 457). Not only is technology under capitalism revolutionary *per se* but it also has profound social and economic effects.

One of the foremost of these is the impact of machine production on petty production. In one of Marx's typically striking one-liners that capture the essence of some particular phenomena, he notes: 'So long as, in a given branch of industry, the factory system extends itself at the expense of the old handicrafts or of manufacture, the result is as sure as is the result of an encounter between an army furnished with breach-loaders, and one armed with bows and arrows' (*Capital*, I, p. 424). In drawing attention to the inescapable demise of petty production in the branch of industry where machinery is introduced, Marx at the same time, carefully notes that it need not immediately apply to other sectors of production, where production based on petty production or manufacture may indeed increase.

However, the spread of machinery across different sectors of production in any country (and increasingly across the globe under latter-day capitalism and imperialism) is a complex process, with many contingent factors that affect the actual nature of the transformation. As Marx notes, the immediate impulse and the proximate cause for the actual diffusion of machinery can vary across different countries and would include competition, shortage of labour or even the need to defeat and subdue a recalcitrant working class.[11]

In reading Marx's account of the revolutionary transformation of the productive forces under capitalism, one must not infer that Marx intended to mean this as a story of inevitable technological progress unaffected by other conditions. As Marx notes: 'No capitalist ever voluntarily introduces a new method of production, no matter how much more productive it may be, and how much it may increase the rate of surplus-value, so long as it reduces the rate of profit. Yet every such new method of production cheapens the commodities' (*Capital*, III, p. 264). Marx adds: 'As soon as the new production method begins to spread, and thereby to furnish tangible proof that these commodities can actually be produced more cheaply, the capitalists working with the old methods of production must sell their product below its full price of production, because the value of this commodity has fallen, and because the labour-time required by them to produce it is greater than the social average. In one word—and this appears as an effect of competition—these capitalists must also introduce the new method of production, in which the proportion of variable to constant capital has been reduced' (p. 265).

The first part of the quote illustrates two points that are essential to understanding Marx accurately. The first is that historical materialism in Marx's hand is not some system of historical pre-determination. In the real, empirical world, the laws of motion of capitalism are realised in concrete conditions. Thus the manner in which the fundamental laws are realised in particular historical conditions may vary and require further study. So would the behaviour of individual capitalists, or the bourgeoisies of particular nations. The laws of motion of capitalism are not reducible to statements about the behaviour of such individual groupings.

At the same time, the empirical manifestations of any law or general tendency have to be worked out concretely, taking into account the development of the fundamental 'cell' of the capitalist mode of production and its contradictions into a full fledged capitalist economy, and it is to this task that the second and third volumes of *Capital* are devoted.

THE CONTRADICTORY CHARACTER OF TECHNOLOGY
UNDER CAPITALISM

Marx's writings on machinery and industrialization have had a definite influence on mainstream economic theory.[12] However, this interest is largely confined in an isolated way to Marx's remarks on technology per se. But in Marx's own writing, technology is always discussed with reference to the social and economic context, namely the capitalist mode of production.

The difference between the one-sided readings of Marx and Marx's own 'dialectical' (to give it its correct name) view is captured well by the concluding resolution of the same meeting of the General Council of the International Workingmen's Association that we had referred to earlier, passed on the day after Marx's intervention, which notes that:

'on the one side machinery has proved a most powerful instrument of despotism and extortion in the hands of the capitalist class; . . . on the other side, the development of machinery creates the material conditions necessary for the superseding of the wages-system by a truly social system of production.'

In what manner does machinery set the stage for the overcoming of the wages-system?[13] Marx summarizes the argument as follows:

It destroys both the ancient and the transitional forms, behind which the dominion of capital is still in part concealed, and replaces them by the direct and open sway of capital; but thereby it also generalises the direct opposition to this sway. While in each individual workshop it enforces uniformity, regularity, order, and economy, it increases by the immense spur which the limitation and regulation of the working-day give to technical improvement, the anarchy and the catastrophes of capitalist production as a whole, the intensity of labour, and the competition of machinery with the labourer. By the destruction of petty and domestic industries it destroys the last resort of the 'redundant population' and with it the sole remaining safety-valve of the whole social mechanism. By maturing the material conditions, and the combination on a social scale of the processes of production, it matures the contradictions and antagonisms of the capitalist form of production, and thereby provides, along with the elements for the formation of a new society, the forces for exploding the old one. (*Capital*, I, Ch. 15, p. 472)

Thus, on the one hand technology revolutionizes production, constantly sweeping lower forms of production away (and on this aspect there is no element of nostalgia for the past in Marx, in contrast to a significant body of writing on technology). Nevertheless as a consequence, technology also aggravates the general crisis of capitalism that ultimately originates in the tendency of capitalism to overproduction.

Marx's analysis of technology is distinguished by the fact that it is situated within the framework of how capitalism can be transcended, or rather how the internal contradictions of capitalism themselves make its eventual supersession necessary. But as Marx illustrates in *Capital*, the point is neither to be made simply by assertion nor by the rejection of science. In the sense of a science, Marx's work emphasises that one has to demonstrate in the empirical world the consequences of the contradictory aspects of reality that we are referring to. At the same time, as Marx does so energetically throughout *Capital*, it is also necessary to rebut the apologetics that mainstream economic theory calls forth to cover up the reality of capitalism, especially in its impact on the majority of the working class.

From the general body of Marx's work, it is clear that the two chapters of the first volume of *Capital* are part of a detailed and extensive study of technology, presented not only in these two chapters but also in a number of passages in other works such as the *Grundrisse*, etc.[14] Some of these passages contain more insights or consider some issues in greater detail. For instance, Marx writing elsewhere on the fundamental contradiction of technology under capitalism, notes how technology under capitalism in the manner in which it develops social production constantly reduces necessary labour time and yet necessary labour time remains the fundamental measure of value under capitalism. It must also be remembered that Capital, and some of the associated works, are primarily writings in political economy. But there are a number of other works that explore in greater detail the political and social implications of technology under capitalism.

SCIENCE & TECHNOLOGY IN THE ERA OF IMPERIALISM – BRIEF REMARKS & CONCLUSION

Utilising Marx's insight in the contemporary world of course implies that we must take into account the fact that capitalism has evolved to the stage of monopoly capital and imperialism.[15] In the second half of the twentieth century, imperialism suffered a series of defeats and a number of nations acquired national independence in a massive wave of decolonization. At the same time, through the second half of the twentieth century, the achievements of socialism in the Soviet Union powerfully determined the economic, social and political context in which the newly-independent nations sought to advance their industrialization. A critical difference among these nations is of course the fact that a few undertook industrialization under the political hegemony of the working people, such as China, Vietnam, etc., while others did so under the hegemony of capital in alliance with the non-capitalist exploiting classes. These considerations are essential to understanding the path to industrialization in these countries and the role of technology and technological advance in this respect.

The development of monopoly capital is the inevitable result of the concentration of production under capitalism, which Marx noted as one of chief characteristics of later capitalist production.[16] Under monopoly conditions, competition is restricted to a smaller number and yet it grows ever more fierce. This has its effect on technological advance too, one of the inevitable consequences of competition.

On the one hand, monopoly is sought to be preserved by means of restricting the spread of technical knowledge. Especially from the latter half of the twentieth century onwards, patents, copyright and various other such legal strategies have become increasingly important as part of the armoury of competition. Patents cease to be a means of ensuring that technical knowledge becomes available to all sections of capital as in an earlier era (albeit with some return to the one who has seized control of such knowledge – note that he need not have invented it) and is increasingly used as a means of restricting competition. At the same time, competition constantly breaks out anew nevertheless, with new scientific knowledge being the means to break the monopoly.

If in the earlier phase of capitalism, science was first separated from labour, nevertheless the universal labour that is science,[17] is increasingly important to production. This leads on the one hand to attempts to appropriate for private use the product of the universal labour of science, significantly intensifiying the contradiction between the universal character of scientific knowledge and its appropriation for the profits of monopoly capital. It also increasingly brings the universal labour of science closer to the character of co-operative labour as in the case of production. The desperation of monopoly capital in attempting to preserve its knowledge monopoly in contemporary times can stretch to the limit of requiring the scientific personnel who have worked for them to not work for anyone else (at least for a limited period)—in other words a direct limitation of the freedom of the scientific worker to sell his labour power, at least for a brief period of time. Nevertheless, no such restriction can clearly work indefinitely.

Monopoly capital in the imperialist nations also seeks to restrict the competition posed by capital from the newly independent nations by seeking to impose a global economic order that attempts to subordinate the Third World. And yet in attempting to benefit from the international division of labour, it must allow the spread of industrialization and the diffusion of technical knowledge. Monopoly capital has little concern for the working class of the nation of its origin in the process, and the constant search for lowering the costs of production drives it to locate production physically in other nations. In doing so, retaining control of its monopoly of scientific and technical knowledge becomes ever more important. At the same time, the more advanced techniques of production relocated in the Third World, even if originally obtained under conditions of subordination, constantly decimates the weaker and more backward forms of production in these nations, setting the stage for them to emerge as competitors to the advanced capitalist nations, with a few indeed having succeeded to an extent in doing so.

In all this, the enormous potential of the advance of knowledge to improve the welfare of the majority remains always underutilised or ignored. Inter-imperialist rivalry in its most extreme form was the driving cause of two world wars in the last century. Superiority in the battlefield was often sought through technological advance. The rivalry with the first socialist state drove this battle for technological superiority to ever higher levels. Despite the collapse of the first socialist experiment, the imperialist nations continue to spend enormous amounts on technology for war.

Let us end with some remarks on the question of the environment. Marx (and Engels) noted that capitalism is founded on the continuing exploitation of natural resources and labour. Capitalism as Marx noted, introduces a radical discontinuity in the 'metabolic' processes associated with cultivation, by transporting agricultural produce and waste to far-removed locations, such that the nutrients removed from the soil in one location are never returned to that location again. At the same time, the industrial revolution also turns attention to the use of waste, utilising waste from some industrial processes in the production process where possible.[18]

It must be noted that the problem has turned acute only in an era subsequent to Marx's time. But mainstream environmentalist views have always had the ghost of Malthus keeping them company in the background.[19] If not Malthusian, environmentalist views tend to be one-sidedly pessimistic regarding technology. However, the continued despoilation of the environment can clearly undercut the conditions of production themselves, whether in agriculture or industry. This problem that was originally thought to be local, now turns out to have a global dimension too, to the extent that (if current scientific estimates hold true) even species well-being may be seriously compromised. It is also interesting to note that typically bourgeois environmentalism has served to undo the 'mystical' element, typical of the early environmentalists, placing questions such as the valuation of economic resources and the assignment of property rights to environmental resources firmly on the economic agenda.

In relation to Marx, the common critique has been that his technological optimism is one-sidedly 'productionist', whereas the environmental question really needs an understanding of the problem of consumption and the manner of regulating and controlling it. Marx's view of the 'metabolic rift' shows that this criticism is misplaced.[20] In relation to the study of capitalism, to accuse Marx of 'productionism' is akin to blaming the messenger for the message.

Marx's analysis underlines the importance of the social control of production if technology is to benefit and answer human needs. Will the continued domination of capitalism result in the conditions of production to be damaged to such an extent as to endanger even species survival? The answer to this question lies in the future. But what Marx's viewpoint would point to unambiguously is the fact that any solution to environmental questions in the framework of capitalism would entail fresh burdens on the working people of the world. And it is certainly true that the socialization of the ownership of the means of production would also firmly place environmental resources in the domain of social ownership.

In conclusion, the argument of this note is not that Marx and Engels and their work provide in any sense a complete answer to understanding the contradictory nature of technology under capitalism. Especially in the study of an evolving mode of production that is made by human actions, 'though not undertaken in circumstances of their own choosing', no such claim would be tenable. However, without doubt, Marx's analysis of the 'law of motion' of capitalist society as well his stand, viewpoint and method are indeed critical in the search for such an understanding.

NOTES

1 F. Engels, 'Speech at the graveside of Marx', available on the web at http://www.marxists.org/.

2 Engels also refers in the speech to Marx's interest in the work of the French engineer, Marcel Deprez, who at that time had argued for an electricity distribution system and had just the year before practically demonstrated the transmission of electricity over long distances.

3 Marx, 'On the Consequences of using Machinery under Capitalism', *Collected works of Marx and Engels*, Vol. 21; available on the web at http://www.marxists.org/.

4 Some of these steps are discussed in Prasenjit Bose's contribution to this volume.

5 All references to *Capital* are from the LeftWord Books edition, New Delhi, 2010.

6 Notable exceptions include the economic historian Nathaniel Rosenberg, among non-Marxists, and the Soviet philosopher Evald Ilyenkov among Marxists. See N. Rosenberg, 'Marx as a student of technology' in *Inside the Black Box: Technology and Economics*, Cambridge University Press, Cambridge, 1982 and E.V. Ilyenkov, 'The Materialist Conception of Thought as the Subject Matter of Logic' in *Dialectical Logic*, Progress Publishers, Moscow, 1977.

7 See Eric Hobsbawm, 'Asking the Big Why Questions: History: A New Age of Reason', *Le Monde Diplomatique*, December 2004.

8 As many readers of Marx are aware, his *Economic and Philosphical Manuscripts of 1844* have some eloquent descriptions of this transformation, but reading *Capital* is essential to understanding how this transformation takes place.

9 The classic study in this regard in the era of contemporary capitalism is undoubtedly Harry Braverman, *Labour and Monopoly Capital: The Degradation of Work in the Twentieth Century*, Cornerstone Publications, Kharagpur, 2006. Some critics of Braverman, for instance Gavin Mackenzie, have however suggested that the analysis tends to one-sidedly overemphasise the aspect of de-skilling of labour by technology. See Mackenzie, 'The Political Economy of the American Working Class', *The British Journal of Sociology*, Vol. 28, No. 2 (June 1977).

10 Of interest in this connection is the literature on the phenomenon of death due to over-work in present-day Japan, known as Karoshi. According to a Japanese trade union confederation, many more workers suffer from acute stress, amounting to more than 53 per cent of the population. For a recent media account of the phenomenon, see Catherine Makino, 'Death from Overwork persists Amid Economic Crunch,' available on the net at http://ipsnews.net/news.asp?idnews=49047

11 Letter from Marx to Pavel Vasilyevich Annenkov, 1846, available on the net at http://www.marxists.org/archive/marx/works/1846/letters/46_12_28.htm

12 A very good example of this, with many insightful comments, is in the work of Nathan Rosenberg, various books and essays. One interesting question that Rosenberg raises is whether Marx underestimated the uncertainity and risk associated with the development of new technology. It would appear though that Marx certainly recognized it but it is not a theme that he appears to have explored at length.

13 Marx undoubtedly is making reference here to the supersession to the relations of production under capitalism and the wording is necessitated by the fact that it is a resolution by the General Council of the International.

14 Some of the relevant works are the *The Grundrisse, The Production Process of Capital*, and *Results of the Direct Production Process*, all available on the web at http://www.marxists.org/archive/marx/works/subject/economy/index.htm.

15 Needless to say, Lenin's tract, *Imperialism, the Highest Stage of Capitalism*, is indispensable reading in this respect. This is also available from LeftWord Books.

16 The following short summary titled 'Three cardinal facts of capitalist production' appears at the end of chapter 15 of *Capital*, III, p. 266:

1) Concentration of means of production in few hands, whereby they cease to appear as the property of the immediate labourers and turn into social production capacities. Even if initially they are the private property of capitalists. These are the trustees of bourgeois society, but they pocket all the proceeds of this trusteeship.

2) Organisation of labour itself into social labour: through co-operation, division of labour, and the uniting of labour with the natural sciences.

In these two senses, the capitalist mode of production abolishes private property and private labour, even though in contradictory forms.

3) Creation of the world-market.

The stupendous productivity developing under the capitalist mode of production relative to population, and the increase, if not in the same proportion, of capital-values (not just of their material substance), which grow much more rapidly than the population, contradict the basis, which constantly narrows in relation to the expanding wealth, and for which all this immense productiveness works. They also contradict the conditions under which this swelling capital augments its value. Hence the crises.

17 See for instance the brief remarks at the end of Ch. 5 in *Capital*, III, in the section titled 'Economy through Inventions.'

18 Among the most comprehensive overviews of Marx's views on ecology related questions is undoubtedly John Bellamy Foster, *Marx's Ecology: Materialism and Nature*, Monthly Review Press, New York, 2000.

19 The much-cited essay by Garrett Hardin, 'The Tragedy of the Commons', *Science*, Vol. 162, p. 1243-1248, 1968, for instance, is despite its fame, an offensively Malthusian tract.

20 See Foster, *Marx's Ecology*.

A Marxist Perspective
on the World Economy

Prabhat Patnaik

In Volume I of *Capital* Marx draws a picture of the capitalist economy where wages are at some historically determined subsistence level. Marx of course sees the level of wages as fluctuating in absolute terms, in accordance with the variations in the size of the reserve army of labour relative to the active army; but it is reasonable to assume, though Marx does not explicitly say so, that as long as the relative size of the reserve army is above a certain *threshold level,* fluctuations in this relative size which occur *above this level,* will scarcely have much impact on the real wage. Hence unless the pace of capital accumulation is such as to bring the relative size of the reserve army below this threshold level, the real wage will continue to remain at the subsistence level and any increase in labour productivity, provided no problem of deficiency of aggregate demand arises, will simply accrue to the capitalists as profits. Even an iota of productivity gain under these circumstances will not percolate down to the workers.

This however has not happened historically in the advanced capitalist economies. As labour productivity has increased in these economies, real wages have also gone up, so much so that all 'growth models' in 'mainstream' economics have been obliged, for the sake of historical verisimilitude, to yield the conclusion that the wage share remains constant over time (which has been considered one of the 'stylized facts' about capitalism). How could wages go up with labour productivity in the advanced capitalist countries, even though there were massive labour reserves in the underdeveloped world? Or putting it differently, even though the relative size of the reserve army located *within* the advanced countries might have been somewhat limited, for the world economy as a whole, i.e. *taking the advanced and the backward economies together,* the reserve army was enormous. How then do we explain the success of the workers in the advanced capitalist countries in enforcing real wage gains in consonance with productivity increases?

The answer to this question lies simply in the fact that *historically the world economy was a segmented one.* Labour was not free to move from the backward to the advanced economies. What is more, even the belt within which labour was free to move from the backward economies and the belt within which labour moved from the advanced economies were kept strictly separate. Thus Arthur Lewis talks about two separate streams of migration in the nineteenth century which were kept strictly separate from one another: a stream of migration from Europe to the temperate regions of white settlement, such as the United States, Australia, New Zealand and Canada, and a stream of migration from the tropical colonies and semi-colonies like India for work as indentured labourers or coolies in plantations in the West Indies, Fiji, Mauritius and parts of Africa.[1] None belonging to the latter stream could stray into the former stream.

Migration of capital from the advanced to the backward economies, which could play a role similar to the migration of labourers in the opposite direction in equalizing wages, was also limited. Capital migration occurred for the development of mining and plantation sectors in the backward economies for export to the metropolis, but not for setting up manufacturing units in these economies, using the same technology as in the metropolis, to take advantage of their lower wages. This reluctance of capital to move from the metropolis to the backward economies, except to specific sectors like minerals and plantations, has been variously explained;[2] but it remains nonetheless a puzzle, indeed the central puzzle in the explanation of the division of the world into a developed and an underdeveloped segment.

This absence of free capital mobility from the metropolis to the backward economies was reinforced by restrictions placed on the bourgeoisie of the latter economies in setting up manufacturing units within these economies, using the same technologies as in the metropolis with locally available cheap labour, for the purpose of exports.[3] From the absence of 'infant industry' protection, to the denial of credit from a banking system controlled by metropolitan capital, to the placing of restrictions (in the form of high tariffs) in the metropolis on manufactured goods exports from the backward economies (restrictions that did not exist when it came to primary commodity exports), a plethora of obstacles was placed in the way of the domestic bourgeoisie of the backward economies (at least in the pre-First World War period) to ensure that it could not challenge the near monopoly position of metropolitan capital in manufacturing activities.

Hence, through various means, the world economy was kept completely segmented. Labour *could not move* from the backward economies to the metropolis; capital *did not move* from the metropolis to the backward economies (except to mines and plantations); and competing local capital was not allowed to come up. A pattern of international division of labour thus got institutionalized, with the metropolis producing manufactured goods and the periphery primary commodities. Wage differences persisted and widened between these two segments, giving rise, as many have argued, to a system of unequal exchange. The advanced country workers in these conditions could get the benefit of labour productivity growth, being insulated, as it were, from the baneful consequences of the massive third world labour reserves (which were themselves created through the processes of 'de-industrialization' and 'drain of surplus' unleashed by the imperialism of the metropolis).

II

Neo-liberalism however has changed all this. While restrictions continue to be placed on the migration of labour from the 'south' to the 'north', capital, in the form both of free-floating finance and of direct investment by multinational corporations, is far more mobile across the world today than it has ever been. What is more, the neo-liberal regime instituted under the hegemony of international finance capital has also entailed the removal of restrictions on the exports of non-primary commodities from the 'south' to the 'north'. Under these circumstances the old segmentation can no longer persist in the world economy which will have to move closer and closer (in an ideal sense) to the Marxian picture of capitalism drawn in Volume I of *Capital.*

Two very obvious implications follow from this. First, it becomes impossible now for wages in the metropolis to be insulated from the baneful consequences, the downward drag, exerted by the massive labour reserves of the backward economies. And, as the real wages of the metropolis become subject *ceteris paribus* to a tendency to move towards the historically-determined subsistence wages prevailing in the backward economies, the labour productivity in the backward economies becomes subject *ceteris paribus* to a tendency to move up towards the labour productivity level of the metropolis. What this means *inter alia* is that even abstracting from technological progress, i.e. any shift in the existing frontier technologies, the share of surplus in world output has a tendency to increase.

Secondly, this tendency towards a rise in the share of the surplus in world output becomes even stronger with technological progress. Since technological progress typically increases the level of labour productivity in the world economy as a whole, the fact that wages do not increase in tandem because of being linked to the massive labour reserves that exist in the world economy entails a rise in the share of surplus. Sweezy had based his theory of underconsumption precisely on this picture of the capitalist economy drawn by Marx in Volume I of *Capital*.[4] If the reserve army keeps the wage rate tied to a subsistence level then any increase in labour productivity accrues *ex ante* as surplus to the capitalists, and hence creates a problem of realization: for its realization there has to be larger and larger demand either from capitalists' consumption, or from 'wasteful' expenditure on account of unproductive labourers (lawyers, advertisers, public relations experts and such others whose sustenance enters on the cost side of output), or from capitalists' investment, or from the State.

Both these phenomena, namely the tendency towards a rise in the share of surplus within the existing set of technologies and the tendency towards a further rise caused by technological progress in the face of non-increasing (and indeed, on the average, declining) level of real wages in the world economy, thus give rise conjointly to an acute problem of realization.

III

Now, if there is a realization crisis, i.e. the surplus is not fully realized in the form of profits owing to the deficiency of aggregate demand, and hence gives rise to unemployment and unutilized capacity, then this unemployment and unutilized capacity typically will affect predominantly the advanced countries. This is because, notwithstanding the *tendency* for advanced country wages to move towards the subsistence level of wages prevailing in the backward economies, in any given period they still continue to be higher than these subsistence wages. In short, wage adjustment occurs in a sluggish fashion, so that the advanced country products tend to have higher unit costs than the backward country products when the same technology is used in both places. Advanced country producers therefore become the 'marginal producers', and the brunt of any inadequacy of aggregate demand falls upon them.

Putting it differently, backward countries need do nothing to overcome the problem of world deficiency of aggregate demand, since they would not be affected by it (if they are more or less producing the same products, using the same technology, as the advanced countries): being low-wage economies, they have an infinitely elastic demand for their exports. It is the advanced countries which have to bear the brunt of unemployment and unutilized capacity in the event of a deficiency of world aggregate demand, and have to take measures against it.

But no matter what measures they take, or even whether they take any measures at all, the sheer tendency for a rise in the share of surplus in world output (for both the reasons mentioned above) *will necessarily have the effect of causing a current account deficit in the advanced country balance of payments.* The reason is simple and can be seen as follows.

Let us imagine a world with only two economies, advanced and backward, with the former having a higher level of real wages than the latter. Starting from some initial situation, let us suppose a new technology becomes available which entails a higher labour productivity and which therefore is used in both economies. Since the real wages in the backward economy remain at the subsistence level, even as labour productivity rises, it faces *ceteris paribus* a deficiency of aggregate demand at the old output (because the number of workers employed and hence the magnitude of workers' consumption will go down at this level of output). But because it is the lower cost producer, it can always get around this problem of deficiency of aggregate demand through larger exports. Hence the reduction in workers' consumption in this economy is counterbalanced by a rise in export surplus, and employment and capacity utilization remain unchanged compared to the initial situation. The advanced country thus faces a deficiency of aggregate demand at its old output for two reasons: the decline in its workers' consumption (because wages do not rise with productivity) *and the export surplus from the backward economy.* Now, no matter what it does to overcome this deficiency, and no matter how much of this deficiency is actually overcome, the export surplus from the backward economy, and hence a current account deficit for the advanced country, must continue to remain. This current imbalance in short is thrown up by the tendency towards underconsumption in the world economy.

This has a direct bearing on the current world scenario. Much has been written about the growing current account deficit of the US, and in particular its growing deficit vis-a-vis China. This growing deficit, as can be easily seen by substituting 'China' and 'the US' in the above example for the 'backward' and 'advanced' economies, is merely a fall-out of the tendency towards underconsumption in the world economy which arises because of the universal institutionalization of a neo-liberal regime.

This universal institutionalization, imposed paradoxically by the diktat of imperialism led by none other than the US itself, serves the interests of international finance capital, which now enjoys the freedom to roam all over the world in quest of speculative gains, and of large multinational corporations which can now locate their plants anywhere. But it is damaging to the interests of the workers in the US itself who have to face growing unemployment and a downward pressure on their real wages even as their labour productivity increases. And together with this there is also an increase in the US current account deficit. The US economy in short faces a triple crisis in the process of serving the interests of its big financiers and corporations: declining real wages, growing unemployment, and rising current account deficit (and with it increasing external indebtedness). And these crises have nothing to do with the current recession; they exist independently of it, with the recession being superimposed upon them.

True, when the recession began, the US had very low levels of unemployment, but that was because of the housing 'bubble' which had temporarily camouflaged the underlying triple structural crisis. In other words the 'bubble' was superimposed upon it, just as the recession following the bursting of that 'bubble' currently is. But these superimpositions must not blind us to the underlying structural crisis arising from this particular feature of neo-liberalism, namely the linking of real wages all over the world to the massive labour reserves existing in the backward economies. (There are of course other major features of neo-liberalism causing other kinds of crisis which are of great significance, but we shall not dwell upon them in this paper).

IV

It may be thought that the de-segmentation of the world economy following the pursuit of neo-liberal policies everywhere, while raising the unemployment rate in the advanced countries compared to its earlier level, will have the opposite effect of lowering the unemployment rate in the backward economies. Putting it differently, even if the labour reserves in the world economy as a whole do not decline relative to the size of the active army employed by capital, *the location of these labour reserves will alter*, with larger reserves in the advanced countries and smaller reserves in the backward countries than before. In such a case, while the workers in the advanced countries will be worse off than before, owing to both lower real wages and higher unemployment rates, those in the backward countries will be better off: their real wages may remain unchanged (since the relative size of the world labour reserves, or even of the labour reserves of these countries alone, may not decline below the threshold level referred to earlier), but their unemployment rates will come down. The universal pursuit of neo-liberal policies then will appear to be of benefit to the backward countries.

There is however an additional factor to be considered here. Since the share of economic surplus relative to output rises in the backward economies, the rich to whom this surplus accrues spend more relative to the total output. Typically however, their spending takes the form of emulating life-styles prevailing in the advanced countries, and these entail high-labour-productivity activities. The rise in the share of surplus therefore entails a rise in labour productivity, and is employment-curtailing for this reason. (This change in lifestyle involving a shift from more employment-intensive activities to less employment-intensive activities is analogous to the process of 'deindustrialization' of the colonial period under which locally-produced goods had been replaced by imported goods). This fact contributes towards preventing a reduction in the relative labour reserves in the backward economies.

Looking at the matter differently, we can distinguish between three different kinds of labour productivity growth that occur in the backward economy. There is labour productivity growth which occurs because of technological progress, i.e. a shift in frontier technologies, which affects both the advanced and the backward countries. There is labour productivity growth which arises from the shift of activities *from* the high wage advanced country *to* the low-wage backward country. And finally there is labour productivity growth that arises from the lifestyle shifts within the backward country, e.g. the introduction of shopping malls, etc. This last kind of productivity growth arises from the fact that products which already exist in the advanced country but which did not exist earlier in the backward countries and are now introduced, and these typically entail higher labour productivity.

The first of these has nothing to do with any exhaustion of labour reserves in the world economy or in the backward economy. We can abstract from it in the current discussion. It is the second, associated with the shift of activities from the advanced country to the backward country which may involve a decline in labour reserves in the latter. But the decline in labour reserves, associated with this second mechanism of labour productivity increase, may get negated by the effects of the third kind of productivity increase, in which case no reduction in the relative labour reserves may occur at all in the backward economy, and hence no question of any exhaustion of labour reserves.

To take an example, suppose in the absence of any shift of activities from the high-wage advanced countries to the low-wage backward countries, technological progress in the world economy would have raised labour productivity everywhere to just such an extent that, given the vector of output growth rates, the rate of growth of labour demand everywhere would have been zero (this is just a convenient assumption to ignore this particular problem altogether). Now, suppose the shift of activities, raises the growth of labour demand in the backward country and lowers it in the advanced country (entailing zero net employment increase in the world on account of such a shift). Suppose the rate of growth of labour demand on account of this factor in the backward economy happens to be á per cent. But if the rate of contraction in labour demand arising from the structural change in the backward country, owing to the changing lifestyle of the rich, happens to be â per cent, then any reduction in the relative size of the reserve army of labour in the backward economy will occur only if (á-â) exceeds n, the rate of growth of the work-force in the backward country. *The values of the three variables however may well be such that the relative size of the reserve army in the backward country does not decline, even as the relative size of the reserve army in the advanced country increases.* In such a case, even as the workers' condition in the advanced country becomes worse, it does not improve in the backward country either, and may also become worse.

This is not a far-fetched conclusion. If we look at the world economy we find not only that the rate of growth of labour productivity is much higher in the organized sector of high-output-growth economies like India and China than in the organized sector of low-output-growth advanced countries, but also that the difference between output and productivity growth rates in these sectors is no higher in the former than in the latter. On the other hand the rate of growth of work-force is higher in the former than in the latter. Hence, notwithstanding higher output growth in backward countries like China and India, owing to the shift of activities from the advanced countries, the relative labour reserves in the former do not decline even as they increase in the latter (once we abstract from the superimposition of the effects of 'bubbles' and of the collapse of the 'bubbles'). *The pursuit of neo-liberal policies in other words, even though it may lead to a shift of activities from the advanced to the backward countries, and hence to a higher rate of output growth in the latter, worsens the conditions of workers in the former without improving them in the latter; indeed it worsens the conditions of workers everywhere.*

V

This raises an important consideration. Conventional economic theory always emphasizes the benefits of free trade. Its claim is based on the totally unrealistic assumption that there is full employment everywhere. The fact that this claim is completely unfounded is borne out from the experience of the colonized economies which witnessed de-industrialization, unemployment, and the emergence of mass poverty because of being opened up to free trade with the metropolitan economies. But the experience of the colonized economies was part of the segmentation of the world economy which we referred to earlier. In other words, the fact that they experienced deindustrialization and mass poverty was associated with the fact that labour was not mobile from the 'south' to the 'north', that capital did not move from the 'north' to the 'south', and that the local bourgeoisie in the 'south' was not allowed to outcompete the 'north', by producing the same goods as the 'north' was producing and using the same technology, but on the basis of lower wages.

The experience of the neo-liberal era however suggests that even if this particular segmentation is eliminated, free trade still does not benefit the south. True, it leads in the new situation to a shift of activities from the 'north' to the 'south', but it still perpetuates and accentuates mass poverty and deprivation. Or looking at it differently, the generation and expanded reproduction of mass poverty and deprivation is embedded within the dynamics of the capitalist system. Whether there is free trade, or discrimination across regions, only determines where the hiatus emerges: whether it emerges between the metropolitan *economies* and the third world *economies*, or whether it emerges between the bourgeoisie of the metropolitan economy with which the third world bourgeoisie gets integrated more closely, and the workers and the peasants of the third world, towards whose abysmal living standards those of the workers in the advanced countries begin to move.

VI

An amelioration of mass poverty within such a regime requires, logically, the reduction of the relative labour reserves of the world to less than the threshold level discussed earlier. In other words, the prevalence of subsistence wage rates in some economies prevents the increase of wages above subsistence levels in other economies, for then the latter will get outcompeted by the former just as the advanced countries of today are getting outcompeted by low-wage countries like India and China. Hence, no matter how high the output growth rate in a particular third world economy, its wage rate can not increase above subsistence level, unless *world labour reserves are sufficiently lowered*. Indeed even if the labour reserves are exhausted in a particular third world economy experiencing high output growth, its wage rate can still not rise above the subsistence level, for if it did, then the country would still get outcompeted by other, subsistence-wage-countries, just as the advanced countries of today are getting outcompeted, until its output and employment growth rate have dropped, labour reserves recreated within it, and its wage rate fallen back to the subsistence level.

In short, *even a high growth, near-full employment backward country cannot experience a wage rate above the subsistence level until the world labour reserves as a whole have fallen sufficiently (below the threshold level).* And if the pace of technological progress in the world economy is such that this latter situation does not arise, then the workers in all third world economies will forever be stuck at the subsistence level, no matter how successful their economies in terms of growth performance, and no matter how 'miraculous' their growth rates are. Such 'miracles' will only entail larger internal disparities within these countries, but not an improvement in the living standards of the people as a whole. Growth in any country under neo-liberalism, unless the world labour reserves get sufficiently exhausted, can never be 'inclusive'.

The question may arise: even if it is the case that wages will not rise spontaneously until the world labour reserves have fallen below the threshold level, no matter how successful a country happens to be in terms of growth rates of output and employment, why cannot the government in such a country use fiscal means to bring about an improvement in the workers' living standards? The problem here is that in a world economy open to competition, capitalists from different countries are engaged in a Darwinian struggle for survival. The States in these countries support their respective capitalists in this Darwinian struggle. Any measure that improves the condition of the workers and hence increases their bargaining strength, reduces the capacity of the capitalists of that country to withstand this Darwinian struggle. There are strict limits therefore to the extent to which the State in any third world country, even one that is a success story in terms of export and output growth, will help in the amelioration of the conditions of its workers. This is not a matter of invidiousness; it is simply the logic of neo-liberalism which carries forward to the world level the Darwinian struggle among capitalists that Marx had described as characterizing any capitalist economy.

VII

It follows that there can be only two circumstances under which in a world with substantial labour reserves, a country can raise its workers' wages above the subsistence level. The first is if it undertakes an innovation in the Schumpeterian sense. Schumpeter had seen such innovations as being the origin of profits, while Marx had seen such innovations as being a source of *extra profits* that the capitalists undertaking the innovations obtained compared to others. Now, there is of course no reason why the capitalists should share this extra with the workers, giving them a higher than subsistence wage, but in principle it can constitute a source of higher wages in case the workers are in a position to bid away a part of this extra amount. But this extra amount accrues only for a transitional period, until others can copy the innovation, and the quicker it is copied, the briefer is this transitional period.

The second way that wages can rise above the subsistence level is for the country to abandon the neo-liberal regime altogether. The State that can do so will have the ability to affect the internal income distribution in the economy. And the workers in such an economy will have the capacity to bargain for higher wages, since they will not be linked any more to the existence of world labour reserves. In short, since widening income disparities are intrinsically linked to the neo-liberal regime whose hallmark is to tie the wages of domestic workers not just to domestic but to world labour reserves, any control over these disparities, any increase in wages above the subsistence level requires as its pre-requisite a jettisoning of the neo-liberal regime. This is a necessary condition.

Such jettisoning however must be accompanied by an alternative growth strategy, which can only be a domestic-market-oriented growth. The expansion of the domestic market requires above all an increase in the production of the peasant agriculture sector, whose base itself must be widened by the introduction of land reforms. Peasant agriculture does not mean a permanent adherence to petty production. It can encompass the organization of the peasants into co-operative or collective forms, since these forms constitute merely the voluntary coming together of peasants and do not entail the destruction of peasant agriculture, as occurs under capitalism.

Hence, land reforms to widen the base of peasant agriculture, State support to such agriculture (of the sort that existed in India during the *dirigiste* period and whose withdrawal precipitated the agrarian crisis that has claimed 200,000 lives through suicides), an effort to strengthen peasant agriculture by changing its organizational arrangement towards cooperatives and collectives, a process of industrialization based on the home market that is widened through the growth of output in the agricultural sector brought about in this manner, a proactive role of the State in providing a range of welfare services to the people, a judicious restraint on the pace of structural an technological change so that the exhaustion of labour reserves becomes a reality, and, for all this, a delinking from the neo-liberal world economy: these have to be the main components of an alternative growth strategy. Such a strategy can bring together the workers and peasants, since it will benefit not only the workers, through an increase in employment and wages, but also the peasants and petty producers for whom it entails a reversal of the crisis precipitated by neo-liberalism.[5]

VIII

The proposal for a delinking of the economy from the world economy will be objected to by many, since it appears to involve a retreat to nationalism from a regime of globalization. True, globalization is dominated by international finance capital and is carried out under the aegis of imperialism, but the way to fight it, many would argue, is through coordinated international actions by the workers and peasants. Nationalism, even anti-imperialist nationalism, they would hold, represents a retreat from such international struggles, and hence a degree of shutting oneself off from the world which has potentially reactionary implications.

There are two basic arguments against this position. First, internationally-coordinated struggles, even of workers, is not a feasible proposition in the foreseeable future. And when we see the peasantry as being major force in the struggle against imperialist globalization, so infeasible is the international coordination of peasant struggles, that one cannot escape the conclusion that those who insist on such international coordination are altogether oblivious of the peasant question. In other words, any analysis that accords centrality to the alliance of workers and peasants as the means of embarking on an alternative strategy, cannot but see the struggle against imperialist globalization as being nation-based, with the objective of bringing about a change in the nature of the nation-State.

Secondly, as already mentioned, such delinking is essential for bringing about an improvement in the living condition of workers in any country. And the workers who struggle for such an improvement cannot possibly be asked to wait until a new World State has come into being that is favourably disposed to the interests of workers and peasants.

Besides, for reasons that can not be discussed at any length here, the current regime of globalization is coming unstuck. The fact that the advanced country that provides leadership to the capitalist world (the US at present) must run a continuous current account deficit under the present regime implies that its capacity to provide that leadership role cannot last long. At the same time there is no other contender for such a role at present (in this respect the current situation differs from that of the 1930s); and as Kindleberger has argued, the absence of such a world leader makes the overcoming of the crisis difficult. This is in addition to the fact that international finance capital, which is opposed to all State intervention, except in its own interest, will fight against any State activism, including that of the leading country's State, for overcoming the crisis through demand management. It follows then that the present crisis will be a prolonged one, with occasional 'bubbles', as and when they do occur, causing a temporary and partial recovery, and collapses of such 'bubbles' pushing the world economy back into a slump. In the context of this crisis various strategies will be discussed, canvassed, and explored by different countries in response to the demands of the working people in those countries. This provides a setting for a delinking from the crisis-ridden world economy under thralldom to imperialist globalization.

NOTES

1 See Arthur Lewis, *The Evolution of the International Economic Order*, Princeton University Press, Princeton, 1978.

2 See for instance P.A. Baran, *The Political Economy of Growth*, Monthly Review Press, New York, 1957 and A.K. Bagchi, *The Political Economy of Underdevelopment*, Cambridge University Press, Cambridge, 1986.

3 See A.K. Bagchi, *The Political Economy of Underdevelopment*.

4 See P.M. Sweezy, *The Theory of Capitalist Development*, Dobson, London, 1941.

5 We have not discussed in this point in this paper, but it is discussed in U. Patnaik, *The Republic of Hunger and Other Essays*, Three Essays Collective, New Delhi, 2007.

Contributors

VENKATESH ATHREYA is currently Visiting Professor, Tata Institute of Social Sciences, Mumbai and Advisor, M.S.Swaminathan Research Foundation (MSSRF), Chennai. He was earlier Professor of Economics, Bharathidasan University, Tiruchirapalli. He has co-authored, with Djurfeldt and Lindberg, *Barriers Broken* (1990). He has also co-authored, with Sheela Rani Chunkath, *Literacy and Empowerment* (1996). He is also the author/ principal author of several other monographs/books, including *The State of Food Insecurity in Rural India* (2009) and *The State of Food Insecurity in Urban India* (2010), both published by MSSRF and The World Food Programme of the UN.

VIJAY PRASHAD is the George and Martha Kellner Chair in South Asian History and Director of International Studies at Trinity College, Hartfort, Connecticut, USA. He is the author of 11 books, including four for LeftWord: *War Against the Planet: The Fifth Afghan War, Imperialism and Other Assorted Fundamentalisms* (2002), *Enron Blowout: Corporate Capitalism the Theft of the Global Commons* (2002), *Dispatches from Latin America: Experiments Against Neoliberalism* (2006), and *The Darker Nations: A Biography of the Short-Lived Third World* (2009). He writes regularly for a number of journals and websites, including *Frontline, Himal* and www.counterpunch.org.

JAYATI GHOSH is Professor of Economics at the Centre for Economic Studies and Planning, School of Social Sciences, Jawaharlal Nehru University, New Delhi. Her recent books include *The Market that Failed: Neoliberal Economic Reforms in India* (2002, from LeftWord), *Work and Well Being in the Age of Finance* (2003), *Tracking the Macroeconomy* (2006), *Never Done and Poorly Paid: Women's Work in Globalising India* (2009) and *After Crisis: Adjustment, Recovery and Fragility in East Asia* (2009). She was the principal author of the West Bengal Human Development Report 2004 which received the 2005 UNDP Award for excellence in analysis. In addition to her academic work, she is a regular columnist for several newspapers and journals, including *Frontline, Businessline, Asian Age, Deccan Chronicle* and *Ganashakti.*

R. RAMAKUMAR is an economist, with a Ph.D. from the Indian Statistical Institute, Kolkata. His areas of work are agricultural economics, agrarian studies and rural development. He is presently Associate Professor at the School of Social Sciences at the Tata Institute of Social Sciences, Mumbai.

PRASENJIT BOSE holds a Ph.D. in Economics from the Jawaharlal Nehru University, New Delhi. He is the Convenor of the Research Unit of the Communist Party of India (Marxist). He is editor of *Maoism: A Critique from the Left* (2010, from LeftWord).

T. JAYARAMAN is currently Professor and Chairperson, Centre for Science, Technology and Society, School of Habitat Studies at the Tata Institute of Social Sciences, Mumbai. Trained as a theoretical physicist and having worked for several years in that discipline, he has subsequently shifted his academic interests to questions that broadly relate to science and society. His current particular interests include climate change and climate policy, science and technology policy in India including nuclear policy and particular aspects of the philosophy and history of science and technology, with special reference to the Indian context.

PRABHAT PATNAIK has recently retired from the Sukhamoy Chakravarty chair at the Centre for Economic Studies and Planning of the Jawaharlal Nehru University, New Delhi. He is editor of the journal *Social Scientist* and is currently working as the Vice-Chairman of the Kerala State Planning Board. His books include *Whatever Happended to Imperialism and Other Essays* (1995), *Accumulation and Stability Under Capitalism* (1997), *The Retreat to Unfreedom* (2002), and *The Value of Money* (2009).

Also from LeftWord Books

Capital

Volumes I, II, III

Karl Marx

978-81-87496-94-6, pp. 768 + 564 + 960, hardcover

Karl Marx's classic work reissued in a beautifully bound hardcover set from LeftWord.

Volume I
A Critical Analysis of Capitalist Production
Translated from the third German edition by Samuel Moore and Edward Aveling and edited by Frederick Engels
978-81-87496-95-3, pp. 768, HC

Volume II
A Critique of Political Economy
The Process of Circulation of Capital edited by Frederick Engels
978-81-87496-96-0, pp. 564, HC

Volume III
A Critique of Political Economy
The Process of Capitalist Production as a Whole edited by Frederick Engels
978-81-87496-97-7, pp. 960, HC

Special discounts available for Book Club Members. For details of Book Club Membership and to order and pay online via a secure payment gateway, visit **www.leftword.com**. You can also send cheques/drafts in favour of **LeftWord Books** to:

LeftWord Books, 12 Rajendra Prasad Road, New Delhi 110001 INDIA
Phone: (91 11) 2335 9456, 2335 6966